Cozy Mysteries
FROM THE ROCK

A COLLECTION OF SHORT STORIES

Library and Archives Canada Cataloguing in Publication information is available upon request.

ISBN-13: 978-1-77478-197-5

Distributed by:
Engen Books
www.engenbooks.com
submissions@engenbooks.com
First mass market paperback printing: August 2025
Cover Image: © 2025 Ellen Curtis

Cozy Mysteries
FROM THE ROCK

EDITED BY ELLEN CURTIS AND ERIN VANCE

Introduction
Erin Vance

Roughly two decades ago, my younger sister and I would play the Nancy Drew computer games.

I don't expect many others to remember these games: I suspect they had a niche audience. However, my sister and I fell into that audience, and, once we figured out how to play (because those were the days when you had to pay for playthroughs, not just Google them), we each fell into our respective role: I would be the brave one, and my sister would solve the puzzles. There is a rhythm to these games: Act One, the jump-scare, Act Two, the near-death experience, Act Three where it all comes together, and then the climax. One of those jump-scares included a sandbag almost falling on us (I remember my sister shrieking and me calmly taking the computer mouse and directing Nancy to carry on); one of those climaxes involved us getting locked in a sarcophagus with a mummy.

We also, at some point, became pretty good at guessing who the criminal was. Move aside, Hardy Boys; the Vance girls were coming through!

Those memories are ones that both of us cling to with fondness and some embarrassed laughter at our younger selves. Those games gave us hours and hours of sister-time, and probably cemented a bond that remains to this day.

If Her Interactive Nancy Drew games are somewhat formulaic, then so are most mysteries. There's the rule of three, your crew of witnesses, a false lead, a suspicious bystander who is revealed to be innocent, and, of course, the *dénouement* to wrap everything up. These are all marks that a good mystery has to hit; and a Cozy Mystery must have all that, plus the right vibe. There are many parts to this recipe, and it takes a certain amount of talent to create something that tastes recognizable yet still delicious. I applaud those that can do so, and, an even more difficult task, do so within the limits of a short story.

There must be something about the Atlantic Ocean that lends itself to the cozy mystery vibe: *Murder, She Wrote* is set in Maine; *Miss Marple* is set in a cozy UK village. Perhaps it is the small-town atmosphere where everyone knows a person; perhaps it is the older generation that always has a word of wisdom and a spark of snark; perhaps it is simply that in the achingly cold and long winter nights, there is nothing quite like a story to keep the home entertained. It therefore seems only right that Newfoundland and Atlantic Canada also make for the perfect stage for a spot o' tea and a bit of crime.

In the pages following, we present to you suspicious mummers, possibly poisoned teas, mysteriously vanished books, and a couple of cats who know more than they'll ever confess to. There are older detectives, lackluster detectives, grumpy detectives, and ones that are more eager than they are skilled. All of them, however, are best enjoyed with a snack and a hot beverage of your choice, wrapped up in your Nan's handmade quilt.

Erin Vance
Editor

CONTENTS

Erin Vance
Introduction..005

Nicole Little
Prose and Cons..009

Marianne King
Borrowing Trouble...043

Chelsea Bee
Death in Dover..081

Mark Squibb
Murder at the Coffee Shop..106

Ryan Belbin
Allowed In...119

Sharon Hunt
Pineapple Crush and Green Zebras..................................145

Teresita E Dziadura
Murder and Myster-teas..155

Melissa Bishop
Book Club..187

Ali House
Exit Pursed by Murderer..197

Nicole Little

Nicole Little lives in St. John's, Newfoundland. Her YA shared-universe novella, *The Lotus Fountain: A Slipstreamers Adventure*, was released by Engen Books in November 2020 and was shortlisted for the Write Project Book of the Year Award in the same year.

Invited, a horror novelette from Australian Publisher Black Hare Press, was released in July 2023 and Nicole's debut Science Fiction novel, *Roxy Buckles & the Flight of the Sparrow* was published by Engen Books in September 2023.

Her short stories have appeared in twenty-three anthologies. She has won several competitions including the June 2018 Kit Sora prize from Engen Books for her flash fiction piece "Sweet Sixteen;" her short story "Doxxed" placed 3rd in the WritersNL "A Nightmare on Water Street: Scary Story Reading" in October 2018 and her three-sentence horror story, "Tasty Babies" earned her the much-coveted Hell Hare award from Black Hare Press in January 2020.

June 2025 saw the release of the second Roxy Buckles novel, *Roxy Buckles and the Cry of the Falcon*.

Prose and Cons

The first golden rays of sunlight percolated through the dust flecked windows of the Laurel Cove Library as Mabel Smythe peered into the newest box of donations for the annual used book sale. It was quiet for a Tuesday morning, but soon the library would be open for the day and the steady trickle of patrons would add life to the old building.

As Mabel rifled through the donations, she paused occasionally to admire a particular cover, to open it up to read the dedication, to see if it was a signed copy. Sometimes she would sigh and toss a book to one side if it was missing pages or had stains or marks or scribbles.

Some people had no respect for the written word.

Why, just last week she had found a beautiful volume that had been absolutely desecrated.

A footstep behind her broke the silence.

"We aren't open yet ... oh it's you," Mabel remarked, turning around. "What are you doing here?" She smirked. "I've already told you how this is going to go. I'll be in contact again ... soon."

Mabel turned her back, dismissing the would-be borrower; a floorboard creaked behind her.

"Get out. You won't change my mind."

That turned out to be Mabel's final words. After that, everything went dark.

And it stayed that way.

Lottie Banks huffed and puffed down Main Street, her breath misting in front of her face in the brisk morning air. She was nearing the end of her run, having changed her route slightly today so she could stop by the library before heading back home. She crested the hill and slowed her pace to catch her breath.

Last week she signed up for a library card for the first time since she was in elementary school. Not that she didn't like to read — she did, very much so, she just hadn't had the time for many of the things she enjoyed when she lived back in the city. She was still adjusting to small town life but now that she had joined the local book club, she hoped to increase her read pile *and* her circle of friends.

She jogged up the stone steps and pushed her way through the large wooden doors. Even for a library it was eerily quiet. Lottie walked past the main desk and headed for the fiction stacks. Dust motes, put in motion by her passing, floated lazily in a beam of sun.

Lottie had only a vague idea about the book the club was currently reading but she was gung-ho to be a part of it — even if they had already started over a week ago.

She gave a little gasp of satisfaction when she found one lone copy of *Rebecca* languishing on the shelf. She scanned the back cover as she made her way back to the front, looking forward to heading home and curling up in front of the fire.

There was no one at the desk.

She didn't want to call out and incur the wrath of the librarian — everyone knew you didn't shout in a library. But she also didn't want to stand here all day when she had things to do … like starting this book.

Currently unemployed, Lottie didn't really have any other place to be. She was in the process of finding retail space to open a yoga studio. She had worked for a gym before they'd moved but she'd noticed a lack of options here in Laurel Cove (other than a regular gym) and suddenly the dream of being her own boss was a possibility.

Lottie shifted back and forth on her feet, growing impatient.

"Hello?" she called, in a half whisper, still cognizant of where she was.

No response.

She leaned against, almost half across, the circulation desk, craning her neck to peer into the small vestibule behind it.

Wait … was that …

Lottie screamed and, suddenly, the library was no longer quiet and Lottie didn't even care.

Main Street was awash in red and blue. The revolving lights of the police cruisers parked outside the Laurel Cove Library had already drawn a crowd of onlookers who were huddled in small groups across the street.

The owner of *The Daily Grind* wasn't complaining; all

those onlookers needed to keep warm in the chill of the morning, and he was catering them with a steady supply of coffee, tea, and hot chocolate.

Inside the library, Lottie shivered beneath the blanket they had given her after her frantic 911 call summoned first responders. The sheriff was the first to burst through the doors. She was, conveniently, also Lottie's wife, Mae. Lottie threw herself into Mae's arms, sobbing on her shoulder.

"I have to check, Lottie," Mae whispered in her ear. "Just to be sure."

"You can't!" Lottie cried, then lowered her voice. "There's a lot of blood ..."

Mae swallowed, hard. "It's my job, Lottie. I'll be quick."

She was, indeed, quick, ducking in the room briefly and then hurrying back to Lottie. By that time, other members of the small Laurel Cove police force had arrived on the scene. Behind them came an EMT crew. They looked to Mae for direction.

"One, in the office behind the circulation desk," Mae told them. "If you could confirm for me, Danielle, that would be great."

The EMT with a high blonde ponytail nodded their head before ducking behind the desk and in through the small doorway to the office. She returned shortly. "Confirmed."

"Maybe you could take a look at her quickly." Mae nodded in Lottie's direction. "I'm worried about the shock."

And so that's how Lottie found herself covered with

a silver rescue blanket, being handed a glass of water by Ponytail as the police milled about, taking notes, and taking pictures.

Mae came to sit next to her. "I'm going to get one of the guys to take you to the station to give your statement," she said.

"Who's in there?" Lottie asked, without moving.

Mae sighed. "The librarian, Mabel Smythe."

"What happened? Was it an accident?"

"I can't give you details, Lottie; you know that …"

"Oh, come on Mae, I'm not asking for particulars. I found her, I would just like to know how much more freaked out I should be … or not," Lottie replied.

Mae lowered her voice to nearly a whisper. "Definitely not an accident. Someone bashed her head in."

Lottie gasped. "So, I'll be very freaked out then. Did you find the weapon?"

"No, or at least nothing that looks like it was used. You should leave, Lottie; they'll be bringing her out soon enough and you don't want to see that."

"I don't think seeing a body bag will traumatize me much more than seeing an actual dead body," Lottie huffed. There had been so much blood. She'd finally stopped crying and was now trying to stand up, leaving the blanket in a puddle on the chair behind her. "But I'm ready to go. I know it's important, and I want to give my statement while it's still fresh in my mind."

"Okay," Mae responded, waving over one of her deputies. "Ted, Lottie is ready."

After giving her statement, Deputy Ted drove Lottie home.

She desperately wanted a shower, a hot cup of tea, and something to bleach the images from her mind. Every time she closed her eyes, she saw the crumbled body of Mabel Smythe.

She stayed in the shower for longer than was probably acceptable, poured herself a large glass of wine in lieu of tea and sat down with a fresh notebook, curled in a chair by the fire like she had planned all along.

Now that the shock was wearing off, Lottie was starting to get curious. Who would want to murder a *librarian* of all people?

She needed to get her thoughts down on paper.

First, she wrote every single word of the statement she had given to the police, for her own records — she didn't want to forget anything. Secondly, she sketched out a picture of what she had seen, including as much detail as she could. She closed her eyes and this time, allowed the images to play out on the back of her eyelids like a movie.

Her eyes flew open and she groaned. She had remembered something. Something really important.

The copy of *Rebecca*, still sitting on the circulation desk, now a part of the crime scene.

"Lucinda, perhaps a dehumidifier?" Edgar mumbled around a mouthful of egg salad sandwich.

The book club had called an emergency meeting and the ones who were able to make it on short notice were all sitting on the haphazard collection of castoff furniture in Lucinda Stewart's rec room. There were at least seven lamps, none of which did much to illuminate the grim basement; neither did the collection of candles placed around the room.

The candles did nothing to help with the smell either.

Lottie grimaced. *Whose idea had it been to bring egg sand-wiches to the meeting as a snack?* Her stomach rumbled but she was definitely waiting until she got home to eat. She blew across the top of the cup of coffee she had poured from the carafe on a side table. She took a sip and nearly gagged. Gently she placed the cup on the end table beside her, hoping no one noticed. She shifted uncomfortably; the chair she was sitting on had a loose spring that was poking her left butt cheek.

"Let's get down to business," Lucinda said, ignoring Edgar. "We are here to discuss the untimely demise of local librarian and founder of the Big Book Sale, Mabel Smythe. God rest her soul."

Edgar gave a loud harrumph.

"Hush, you." Lucinda admonished. "Mabel was ... well, she was Mabel. But now, with the library closed, that leaves us all in a bit of a pinch. Isn't that right, Lottie dear."

All eyes turned to fix on Lottie.

She cleared her throat, twice. "I had the last copy of *Rebecca* but ... uh ... left it behind, after ... everything. And the place is a ... um ... crime scene now so I can't go back."

Wow. So eloquent. Lottie thought to herself. *Making a great impression here.*

"Was it ... horrible?" asked Katie Rush, one of the English teacher at the local high school. She leaned forward in her chair, not even attempting to hide her eagerness for gossip.

Lottie nodded. "The worst thing I have ever seen."

"Oh my," Lucinda murmured. "You poor thing. Does your lovely wife have any suspects yet?"

Edgar wiped crumbs from his shirt. "It was bound to happen."

Now everyone turned to look at him.

"What?" he asked. "You all know I'm right. Mabel burned bridges like some people burn candles. She finally did it to the wrong person, that's all. I don't believe in all this who-ha about not speaking ill of the dead. Mabel was not a nice person. You know it and I know it."

Lottie tried not to react. Her fingers itched to write this in her notebook. She eyed Edgar with interest.

"Hush, Edgar," Lucinda huffed. "You've had it out for Mabel ever since she turned down your request to use the community room for the book club meetings. My rec room is just as good, if not better."

The elderly man grimaced in response and massaged his knee. He'd been complaining since they got there about the dampness.

"Edgar has a point though, Lucinda," Katie Rush spoke up. "Mabel was a terror. She ruled the library like a dictator. Remember how she wouldn't let me borrow those old copies of *Animal Farm*?"

"Yes, Katie, we all remember," Lucinda replied. Then, under her breath, "You never let us forget."

Katie sniffed indignantly, and picked up an egg sandwich from the table. "They hadn't been borrowed since the eighties! Ridiculous woman." She shoved the triangle whole into her mouth and chewed vigorously, her short brown curls bobbing in time with the motions of her jaw.

Interesting, Lottie thought, furrowing the information away for later.

"Anyways." Lucinda drew out the word, shooting daggers at Edgar and Katie. She turned to Lottie. "Lottie darling, I have an extra copy of *Rebecca* that you can borrow. Be very careful with it though. I don't normally lend out my books but these are special circumstances, you know. No dog ears and please, do not read it in the bathtub!"

"Thank you," Lottie replied. "I really appreciate it! I will take very good care of it."

After that, they discussed what they would do if the police kept the library closed for an extended period of time. Everyone pledged to share the books they had. Not only did the town need a yoga studio but they also, desperately, needed a bookstore.

Lottie was starved.

She let herself into the house; the mouthwatering aroma of butter chicken greeted her along with the excited meows of Monsieur, their slinky black cat.

"Hey, Sir Kitty." Lottie picked the cat up and snuggled him on her shoulder. He turned to purr in her ear.

Mae was in the kitchen. She'd changed out of her work uniform and was now wearing her at home uniform: sweatpants and a hoodie. EarPods in her ears, she was swaying softly while she stirred, humming under her breath. She turned as soon Lottie and Sir entered the room, her police senses picking up on the slight shift in the atmosphere.

Lottie had never been able to sneak up on Mae.

"How was book club?" Mae asked.

"They're an interesting bunch," Lottie replied. "Certainly, no love lost between them and Mabel Smythe."

"Oh really?" Mae perked up.

"Calm down, Sheriff." Lottie laughed. "I just meant, they all had an axe to grind with her, but nothing crazy. Just regular stuff."

"Sometimes it's the regular stuff that gets you killed," Mae replied. "Tell me what you heard."

Lottie couldn't sleep. The butter chicken was heavy in her belly and the murder was heavy on her mind. Mae snored next to her. She had been out like a light before her head hit the pillow.

After flipping her pillow for what felt like the hundredth time, Lottie finally gave up, grabbed an oversized sweater, and slipped out of the bedroom. In her favorite chair, with her favorite blanket, she opened her notebook to a fresh page and began a list of names.

The week went by in a blur of *Rebecca* and rental applications. Lottie had visited a few empty retail spaces; some had been very promising, others had been, well, about as bad as Lucinda's basement. Mae had been working crazy hours; half the Laurel Cove population had been interviewed in some way or another. Even the kid who'd graffitied the library some months ago had been hauled in for questioning.

Today was Friday and Lottie hoped to see her wife for more than a few minutes at a time over the weekend. It was unlikely, but she hoped. She laced up her running shoes and did some stretches on the porch before heading out for her morning run. She hadn't gone back to her old route since that fateful trip to the library, instead, she'd added it most days, jogging past the crime scene slowly, catching her breath and keeping a watchful eye.

She did the same today, slowing her pace; the bright yellow police tape was still in place but the library door was slightly ajar.

Lottie stopped running.

She moved closer towards the front steps of the old building, looked around. There was no one near by.

Before she could change her mind, she bounded up the steps and slipped inside.

It was dark with the overhead lights turned out. Lottie didn't dare turn them on. She took her phone out of her pocket and thumbed the flashlight button. Creeping past the circulation desk, she suppressed a shudder and averted her eyes.

She expected it to be quiet, of course, but it was almost *too* quiet. She tiptoed further into the darkness, trying to keep within the patch of light emanating from her phone.

Deep within the stacks came a thump, and Lottie froze.

She wasn't alone.

Lottie knew she needed to get the hell out of there but there was only one entrance to the library which meant there was only one exit. Her, and whoever else was in here, they both needed to go the same way. Keeping her eyes forward, she walked backwards.

She heard the footsteps pounding towards her before she saw their owner. Dressed entirely in black, they rushed forward, ambushing Lottie. Their shoulders connected with hers and she went flying, phone and flashlight revolving in the air, sending staccato flashes of light over the chaos. Lottie hit the floor hard, but she reacted without thought, throwing out a leg at her attacker. She heard the grunt as her foot made contact, heard the crash as they hit the floor and then a secondary whoosh as something large slid across the floor.

"I've already called the police," her voice was confident, though she didn't feel it. "They'll be here any minute."

The dark figure rose from the ground; Lottie could barely see the shape that loomed above her before they bolted for the door. Lottie collapsed back on the floor, her breathing ragged. She reached out for her phone, easy to find with its beam of light and redirected it around her, searching.

The flashlight swept over something on the floor. Lottie moved closer. It was a book. A large book. She crouched down for a look. It was *The Complete Works of Shakespeare*, a hardcover copy. And it was covered in red blotches.

Lottie was pretty sure she had just found the murder weapon.

With shaking fingers, she dialed her wife's number. Her own personal 911.

After Mae hugged her, she read her the riot act. "You put yourself in real danger, Lottie!" she finally finished.

"I know, I know," Lottie replied, chagrined. "But at least you have the ... you know ... now. It must have been hidden here, and then they came back for it." She gasped. "Do you think they were hiding here, somewhere, when I found the body?"

Mae sighed. "Lottie, leave the investigation to the experts. You could have been hurt."

Lottie shrugged. "At best I have a few bruises. I'm fine, really."

Police were, once again, milling around the library. A few moments ago, the murder weapon had been bagged and taken for analysis. Maybe, if they were lucky, there would be a fingerprint.

"Did you get a good look at them?" Mae asked, her anger dissipating.

"They were wearing a balaclava," Lottie replied. "So, I couldn't see their face, but they were strong. Maybe 5'8" or 5'10," taller than me for sure. I smelled cologne and something else that I can't put my finger on. I'm pretty sure it was a man."

"That's good, Lottie. Anything else you can remember? Did he say anything?"

"No," Lottie said. "He was dressed all in black. Sorry, Mae. I wish I could tell you more."

"You did good," Mae assured her. "That's more than we had before. This will help. Now go home. Stay there and rest."

Lottie took her time walking home.

Once there, she made a coffee, retrieved her notebook,

and stood at the kitchen island, pen in hand. She wrote out everything she could remember, then referred back to the list of names: her suspects. It definitely wasn't Edgar. No way that elderly man would have been able to attack her like that with his bad knee … among his many other ailments. It also ruled out Katie Rush; she wasn't an inch over five feet.

She drew a line through both their names. That left one: Tyler Kent. Tyler was well known around Laurel Cove; Lottie had heard all sorts of stories but the most oft repeated was how Mabel Smyth had him charged with vandalism for tagging the back wall of the library. The teen had gotten probation but he hadn't liked it very much, being volun-told to help out at Golden Heights Manor, the cove's one and only assisted living facility. From what Lottie had heard (because in small towns, there were big mouths), Tyler had been cleaning bedpans and calling Bingo during his time there. Not exactly a teen boy's dream job.

A loud beep from her phone made her jump — it was a reminder to bring her car in for an oil change. A smile crept across her face. She knew Tyler worked part time at the garage. She could kill two birds with one stone.

And, technically, Mae couldn't get mad at her for going out if she was running an errand.

Lottie backed the car into the space provided by Parker Right There Garage. Even if there had been more than one garage in Laurel Cove, Lottie would have chosen this particular place, if for nothing other than its clever name. But she had also been told that Parker Frost, the owner and mechanic, could fix pretty much anything. Lottie drove an old Mazda Miata; she expected that her and Parker would be seeing a lot of each other.

She pocketed the keys and headed inside, keeping her eyes out for any sign of Tyler Kent.

A young woman in greasy coveralls greeted her at the front desk and handed her some forms to fill out. "Parker is running a little behind today, Ms. Banks, but the car should be ready again before we close."

"Thanks, Maggie," Lottie replied, seeing the name embroidered on her shirt pocket. "Just you and Parker working today?"

Nice, Lottie thought, *subtle*.

"Just us," Maggie replied. "Tyler isn't in on Fridays; he volunteers at the assisted living facility over on Hummingbird Lane. You know it? My grandma lives there. Great spot."

"I've driven past it." Lottie smiled. "So, Tyler volunteers there?" She couldn't keep the curiosity, and surprise, out of her voice.

"He does!" Maggie practically beamed. "Tyler's my stepbrother. He got in some trouble last year, ended up doing community service but turns out, he really loves Bingo. He heads over there every Friday afternoon now; hangs out with the oldies, and spends some time with grandma."

"That's ... fantastic," Lottie replied. Inside she groaned. There went the final suspect on her list. It was hard to stay too mad though. Sounded like the kid had landed on his feet and she was happy for him.

"Hey, Maggie, can you call Mr. Richards and let him know his car is all fixed and ready to go?" Parker Frost strolled into the shop, wiping his hands on a rag. He had a streak of grease across his forehead and a cut above his eyebrow. "Oh hello. Ms. Banks? Is that right? Baby blue Mazda Miata?" He grinned.

"Got it in one. Thanks for fitting my car in today, I know you're busy."

"Not a problem. Happy to help," Parker replied.

Maggie jutted her chin at Parker. "Rough night, boss?"

He looked confused for a minute, then laughed. "Oh this." He pointed at his forehead. "Walked into the back bumper of an Escape I had up on the ramp. Hazards of the job."

Maggie laughed. Parker saluted them both and headed back through the door to the garage.

"I should probably give you these." Lottie handed the keys to Maggie, said her goodbyes, and headed out. A brisk walk was just what she needed to clear her head.

She pictured the list she had made, knowing that when she got home, she would strike off yet another name. She was back to square one.

To cheer herself up she decided to grab lunch and drop it off at the station for Mae. She ordered sandwiches, pasta salads, and coffee at *Mom's Diner* and carried the paper bags of good the two short blocks. It was warm inside, which Lottie was grateful for. She saw Mae just inside her office and waved, hoping to grab her attention.

"Hey, I brought you some lunch," Lottie handed the paper cup of coffee to Mae. Mae sipped it gratefully.

"Let's have it in my office. I might be a few minutes, just have to make a quick call to the out-of-state forensics lab but I won't be long. I'm taking the coffee with me though." Mae brushed a kiss on her cheek as she rushed past. "You're the best."

Lottie made her way to Mae's office. It was a mess. She began to tidy the desk, hoping to at least make enough space to put down the food. A folder fell to the floor, spilling its contents, including several large glossy photos. Lottie cursed under her breath and crouched down, trying to cram everything back into the file. She couldn't help but look at the photos, especially when she realized just exactly what was pictured in them.

It was a book. And not just any book either: it was the murder weapon.

Glancing up to make sure she was still alone, Lottie quickly rifled through the file. The book had been photographed from every conceivable angle. But what really got Lottie's attention was what was inside … or rather, what wasn't inside. A large area in the middle of the book had been hollowed out, leaving behind a deep hidden cavity.

It was empty now, of course, but Lottie wondered, just what had been in there that was worth killing for?

She slipped her phone out of her pocket and quickly took pictures of everything in the file, her heart pounding. Mae would kill her if she got caught. But by the time Mae returned to the office, looking harried, Lottie was sitting on the other side of the desk, munching on her club sandwich.

"Sorry," she apologized. "I got hungry."

"Why aren't you at home, resting, like I asked?" Mae

asked, shoving the edge of her ham on rye into her mouth and chewing enthusiastically. "Not that I'm not happy to see you, and the food."

"I had to drop the car at the garage," Lottie declared, happy to have a valid excuse. "I can rest later. I'm fine, I promise. Parker should have it ready by the end of the day."

"One of these days we'll get you something a little more reliable," Mae promised.

"What? How dare you! I love my little car." Lottie grinned. "Look, I know things have been really tight lately, what with the move and me being out of work, but we will get there, babe. Plus, I think I found the perfect spot for the studio."

"Did you really?" Mae's face lit up. "Where? Tell me all about it!"

Before Lottie had a chance to open her mouth, Deputy Ted stuck his head in through the door. "Hey, Sheriff, the lab is on the phone again."

Mae looked regretfully at the rest of her lunch left sitting on her desk, before she rose to her feet. "Sorry, Lottie, I have to go. Give me all the deets later, okay? I love you."

Mae squeezed her shoulder as she walked past.

Lottie cleaned up the mess from lunch and left quietly. Her coffee was cold now but she sipped it anyway as she speed walked the short distance home.

She burst through the door, startling Sir who had been napping on the bench in the porch. She picked him up, planted a kiss on his wee head, and took him with her to the living room. He jumped from her arms onto the couch and regarded her reproachfully.

"Sorry, Sir Kitty."

Grabbing her notebook from its hiding place beneath her favorite chair, Lottie flopped down on the couch next to Sir, and opened the notebook to a blank page. Holding her phone in her hand, finger poised above the photo's app, she felt a pang of guilt. She knew what she had done was wrong, illegal if she was completely honest. She justified it by telling herself that it was for her eyes only, she would never share the information with anyone and, as soon as she figured things out, she'd destroy it.

Satisfied with her plan, she scrolled through the pictures she'd taken of the contents of the file. It was hard to read everything, she'd been in a rush so some were a little blurry. The lab results were pretty clear though. Thankfully. Lottie zoomed in.

They had found evidence under Mabel's nails. She'd tried to fight back. There was DNA.

Lottie tapped her pen against her lips, lost in thought.

Now, all they needed was someone to match it to.

She felt like a bomb went off in her head. She sat up, startling Sir who had, once again, been napping. He opened one eye and gave her a scathing look.

"What if," she said to the cat, who yawned and didn't really seem to care about her bright idea. "What if, when I knocked that guy over, and he dropped the book … maybe whatever was *inside* that pocket came out. And it's just sitting there, somewhere, like under a table, waiting to be found."

She stood up quickly. "I have to get back inside that library."

Mae slipped into bed beside her. "Sorry hun, I thought I'd be home earlier."

Lottie picked up her bookmark and put it between the pages of *Rebecca*. "It's okay. I know you want to catch the guy who did this. Any leads?"

"Not really." Mae punched her pillow. "We're tracking Mabel's steps in the weeks leading up to the murder. She didn't leave the house for much other than work but Mabel Smythe pissed off a lot of people. She was very disagreeable, hostile even. It's not hard to find someone who dislikes her."

"That's kind of sad, don't you think?" Lottie asked.

But Mae was already asleep, softly snoring; Lottie opened her book again. She needed to make sure Mae was out solid before she put her plan into action.

Thirty minutes later, Mae's snores had increased in volume; she hadn't moved once. Lottie eased out of bed and grabbed her hoodie off the dresser. She was already dressed in black leggings and black shirt. She crept down the stairs, hauled on her Doc Martins and quietly let herself out the front door.

Lottie started off at a light jog. She had her cover story ready: she couldn't sleep, so she thought a run might make her tired.

It was a chilly night; Lottie's breath was a continuous mist in front of her, clouding the way towards main street. There were no cars, no other pedestrians. If she really had been out for a midnight run, it would have been perfect.

She could see the library up ahead on her left. The crime

scene tape had finally been removed and it would reopen to patrons on Monday morning with a rotating group of volunteers working there until a new librarian could be hired. Not surprisingly, many people had stepped up to help out, including Lottie.

Lottie did a quick assessment of the area and jogged lightly around the back of the building. Mae had let slip that the back door that led to the basement of the building didn't latch properly. They'd investigated that angle but it seemed like the killer had simply walked right in the front door.

Sure enough, with a bit of wiggling around, the back door creaked open and Lottie let herself in. It was dark. Lottie couldn't see a hand before her. Her heart thumped painfully in her chest.

What in the world were you thinking? she chided herself.

But Lottie knew she was in too deep now. If she could just find whatever had been secreted inside that book, she would pass everything over to Mae and her colleagues and let them do the rest.

Flashlight in hand, she ascended the staircase to the main floor. Her ragged breath seemed far too loud for the tomb-like silence that greeted her at the top. She stepped boldly up to the circulation desk and then dropped to her hands and knees, sweeping the flashlight beneath the desk. Nothing.

"Dammit," she muttered. "Okay, so I was there when he knocked me over, I tripped him here and he fell there." She was trying to map things out in her head. "The book slid towards the stacks …"

She turned in a circle, retracing the steps, picturing in her mind how it all went down.

"Find what you're looking for?"

The deep voice came out of the darkness to her left. Lottie jumped.

"You just can't keep your nose out of things, can you?"

A glimmer of recognition sparked in Lottie's mind. She knew that voice but ... from where?

"I haven't found anything," Lottie replied shakily. "I'll just leave you to it then." She started backing away.

"Not so fast," the man snapped.

"I don't have anything, I swear," Lottie insisted.

"Your wife knows you're here?"

"Yes!" Lottie replied quickly. Perhaps a little too quickly.

The man chuckled. "Somehow, I doubt that. Sheriff Banks wouldn't approve of her wife running wild about town in the middle of the night, getting herself into trouble."

He moved closer. There was that smell again; cologne, yes, but there was that scent beneath it that Lottie was still having difficulty identifying.

There was a click and Lottie's whole body went cold. She didn't have to be a genius to know the man had a gun on her.

"Seems like we are both looking for the same thing. So, let's work together, shall we? I'll supervise, and you find it."

Lottie, who had hated group projects because she always ended up doing all the work, began to frantically sweep the floor with her flashlight. "I don't even know what I'm looking for!" Lottie lamented.

"Then maybe you need to get closer," he snarled.

Lottie felt his foot connect with the back of her knees and she hit the floor — hard. Stifling a cry of pain because she would *not* give him the satisfaction — she gathered herself and started to crawl around, searching under shelves.

"Faster!" he demanded.

Lottie considered the return cart: she could see it out of the corner of her eye and it was chock full of books. If she pushed it hard enough at him, would it take him down? She gave it a tentative shake. It was pretty solid.

But it also seemed to be stuck on something.

She put her head closer to the floor and flashed her light underneath the cart. There was something wedged in the back wheel. Lottie stretched out her arm; it was really stuck in there. Finally, it came loose: a palm size, soft covered, little black book. She flipped through it absent-mindedly, without thinking.

"Give me that!" He bent down and yanked it from her hand.

"Great." Lottie tried to inject some enthusiasm in her voice. "You can let me go now."

He chuckled. "I don't think so."

She sensed something swinging towards her head but had no time to react. Her last thought, before she lost consciousness, was *motor oil*.

When Sheriff Mae Banks awoke that Saturday morning to find that her wife wasn't in bed next to her, she didn't think anything was amiss, especially at first. Lottie would often rise early and go for a run. Her gear was missing from the porch which further solidified this theory.

She made herself a cup of coffee, gave Sir his breakfast kibble, and sat at the kitchen island, scrolling through the messages on her phone. It was supposed to be her day off but Mae knew that was unlikely to happen. In a few hours, if she got that long, she would be back at the station trying to find the person who murdered Mabel Smythe. They just needed that one thing to bust the case wide open. All they had to do now was find it.

Mae was good at her job. She desperately wanted to prove it to the residents of Laurel Cove, to assure them that they did the right thing by hiring her. It was bad enough that there had been a murder on her watch.

Lottie had not returned by the time Mae showered and dressed. Mae tried sending a text: *Babe, u home soon? Xx*

No response.

Now, worry crept in.

Mae paced the living room floor, chewing on a thumbnail. Sir wound himself around her legs, meowing, probably looking for treats.

"Not now, Sir, I'm trying to think." Mae told him.

Sir finally gave up, flopped on the floor by the chair and began playing with something sticking out from under it. Mae squinted, trying to see what it was.

"What have you got there boy?" Mae asked.

Sir meowed at her again, rolled over, hoping for belly rubs. Mae bent down and reached under the chair, and pulled out a slim, floral-patterned notebook. It was filled with Lottie's loopy handwriting. She read through it quickly; the last entry made the hairs rise at the back of her neck.

Lottie had a habit of sometimes getting herself into trouble, poking her nose where it didn't belong, even if she had the best of intentions. Unfortunately, it ran in her blood.

Mae grabbed her phone and placed what she hoped wasn't an overdue call.

"Hey, Ted, yeah, I'm heading in now. But first, I need you to get a start on a missing persons report. No, I'm not joking. It's for my wife, Charlotte Fletcher Banks."

The station was chaotic. Mae wound her way through the desks in the bullpen, entered her office and slammed the door shut. She was frustrated. Still no sign of Lottie and they were no closer to solving the murder than they were a week ago. They'd sent two officers to the library to search for Lottie but it had been deserted.

She had poured over Lottie's notebook for clues, pausing over and over again at the sketch Lottie had made of the man she'd confronted at the library.

She tossed it aside. This was getting her nowhere. Pulling a stack of files towards her, Mae decided she would just start from the beginning and make her way through all the evidence they had collected so far.

She started with the crime scene photos but saw nothing new there. She'd already examined them with a magnifying glass, because she was thorough like that. Then she thought of something. Yanking open the office door, she bellowed for Deputy Ted.

"Ted! Did we get the phone and bank records back from that subpoena yet?"

"Came in on the fax about an hour ago." He walked them straight over to her. "Sorry, we've been a little busy with … other things."

"I know, Ted. And I'm grateful for it," Mae replied.

He nodded at her and went back to work.

Mae sat at her desk, the paperwork spread out in front of her. There wasn't much intel to be gathered from Mabel's phone records. The only places she ever called were a Chinese takeout, her bank, and the garage.

She turned her attention to the banking transactions. Mabel bought a lot of books online. Mae knew the woman owned her home so there were no mortgage payments coming out. All her bills were on autopay and, other than groceries and the occasional takeaway, not much else came out of the account. Her salary was deposited biweekly like clockwork; she appeared to receive a small pension from her late husband's former employer but nothing else was going in.

Except.

Well, that was interesting. There had been a large sum deposited into Mabel's bank account less than a week before her murder. From Parker Frost, the owner of Parker Right There Garage.

Mae jumped to her feet, opened the door and yelled for Ted again. "Ted!" She beckoned him inside the office.

"What did Mabel Smythe drive?"

"She didn't, boss. Mabel didn't have a licence," Ted replied.

"Did her late husband have a car? One she might have sold recently," Mae asked, her voice rising with excitement.

"No. Mr. Smythe had a motorcycle but he sold it himself once he got sick. Why all the questions about cars? You looking to buy, or something?" Ted looked perplexed.

Mae had a look of triumph on her face. "Because Mabel Smythe called Parker Right There *seven* times in the last month, and Parker Frost deposited five thousand dollars into Mabel's bank account the week before she died. Why do you think that is?"

Ted was starting to catch on.

"Grab a patrol car. We're heading to the garage."

Lottie's head was pounding. She groaned against the gag in her mouth and tried to sit up but found, despite her efforts, she could not. Her arms were tied in front of her and her ankles were bound tightly together. Every joint in her body ached in time with the throbbing in her skull.

She *had* to get this stale gag out of her mouth. She pushed with her tongue and rubbed her mouth against the floor, trying to work it loose. It started to move and she gave a triumphant, though somewhat muffled, shout. She continued with her efforts, until finally, she was able to push it all the way out. Her mouth was dry but she gratefully gulped in mouthfuls of stale air.

Next order of business: getting the hell to get out of here. Judging by the smell, she was somewhere inside a garage. She was certain now she knew who had murdered Mabel Smythe and she had a pretty good idea why. She hadn't seen much in that small notebook, but what she had seen, had been enough.

Lottie and Mae hadn't lived in Laurel Cove long but everyone knew about the bus accident in Harbour View, two towns over. The brakes had failed on a school bus taking kids to a field trip; a lot of people had been hurt. A quick glimpse at Parker's log book told her he'd been the one to sign off on the bus, to say that it was safe to be on the road, when it had been anything but.

She pushed the thought from her mind and started to assess the situation at hand. The bindings around her wrists were cloth, maybe a scarf of some type. It was tight, she knew that much. She rubbed it against her face, felt where the knot was, and with no other choice, began to work on it with her teeth. The fear she had originally felt was slowly receding and, in its place, came a seething anger. Tearing at the fabric with her teeth, she finally felt something give. Her hands moved slightly apart. Feverishly, she continued working at the knot, pulling and twisting until her jaw ached. She stopped to catch her breath, yanking her wrists apart to see her progress. She gave a small cheer of triumph; it had loosened just enough to slide a hand through. It hurt like hell but suddenly she was free. She massaged her wrists but quickly turned to the bindings at her ankles. She made fast work of those then lay back on the floor, exhausted.

"No time for this, Lottie," she muttered to herself and stood on wobbly legs. She gave herself a minute to steady and then began to feel along the cold metal walls; surely there had to be a door here somewhere.

Bingo.

Her hands slid across the frame of a door. She fumbled around, searching for the doorknob. There it was!

And lo and behold: it wasn't even locked.

Lottie couldn't work out if Parker Frost was just your typical dumb criminal or if he didn't expect her to be able to escape from her bonds that easily. Either way — she was out of here.

She eased the door open, bright light assaulted her eyes. She blinked, squinted, and peered out into the morning sky. Had she been here all night? Mae must be beside herself with worry. Lottie had no way to tell what time it was. While Parker had taken her phone for obvious reasons, he had also taken her watch.

A sharp shot of pain pierced Lottie's skull. She cringed as her fingers found the large welt at the back of her head: her hair was a mess of dried blood. She swayed, took several deep breaths. She'd deal with this later; right now, she needed to get help, to get to Mae, and to get Parker Frost behind bars for what he had done.

She slipped through the door, keeping close to the outside wall. She was at the back of Parker Right There, the gravel lot where they kept wrecks and old cars for parts. He'd been holding her in a corrugated shed; if the temperatures had dipped last night, she might have frozen to death.

That's probably what he had been what he had been hoping for, Lottie mused.

She crept around the side of the shed, crouched low, trying to make as little noise as possible. If the garage was open, and Maggie or Tyler were there, they might be willing to help her. If their boss was in — Lottie might not even get the chance. Chewing on her bottom lip, she weighed her options. Not willing to walk into what very well could be another trap, Lottie backtracked the way she had come, retracing her footsteps back towards the shed.

That was when she heard the voices.

"Goddammit, Frost. You said you'd taken care of it." It was a deep, gravelly voice. Lottie did not recognize it.

Then Parker spoke: "She was here. She should *still* be here. I told Maggie and Tyler to take the day off. I don't know what the hell happened!"

"What happened is that you're too damned stupid to clean up your own mess. You got us into this, you get us out of it," the other man snarled.

"I *did* clean up the mess, Frank," Parker's voice was full of venom. "I got rid of that meddling old woman, didn't I?"

"Yeah, but you've gone and half-assed it this time, letting this one get away," Frank retorted.

"You know what!" Parker snapped. "Maybe I should cut my losses, turn myself in while I still have a chance. I hear several families are planning to sue the bus company for negligence. The cops might be willing to cut me a deal if I hand over that book."

"Are you threatening me?" Frank asked, his voice flat and cold.

Lottie heard sounds of a scuffle, the slap of flesh as a punch landed and, then, a gunshot. Lottie clamped a hand over her mouth to stifle a scream. Someone moaned and then went quiet.

"Idiot," Frank spat.

Lottie heard him walking away, his feet scuffing across

the crushed stone. She counted to sixty and then risked a look. There was no one around. Parker Frost lay in a tangled heap on the ground and he wasn't moving. Despite everything that had happened, Lottie rushed to his side.

He was still alive. But just.

He was trying to say something. Lottie leaned in closer, her ear was nearly touching his lips.

"Romeo ..." came the faint whisper and then, nothing.

Lottie jumped to her feet and made a run for it. Running was something she was very good at and she wasn't planning to stop until she busted through the doors of the sheriff's office.

She didn't end up getting very far though. As her feet hit the pavement at the front of the garage, a police cruiser pulled up, tires screeching as it careened into the parking lot. Mae was out of the car before it had even fully stopped.

"Lottie, oh my god!" she cried; then over her shoulder she shouted: "Ted, call for an ambulance!"

"Tell it to hurry," Lottie told her. "Parker Frost is out back, he's been shot. I don't think he'll last much longer."

She fell into Mae's arms and began to sob.

Six months later...

"And now, we will finish our practice with Savasana. Lie flat on your back with your legs extended, arms at your sides, palms facing up. Close your eyes and let your body completely relax. Focus on your breath, letting go of any remaining tension in your body. You may remain in this position for as long as you need."

The room was silent except for the soft breathing of the other yogis participating in the sunrise class at *Bliss Yoga Studio*.

Lottie smiled to herself, enjoying the peace and feeling of contentment she always had at the end of a good session.

Suddenly, the silence was broken by a loud rumbling.

"Edgar," Lucinda groaned, slapping the arm of the man just next to her. "Wake up for goodness' sake! You do this every week."

The whole group laughed as poor Edgar tried to come to his senses.

Lottie said goodbye to the motley assortment that joined her early each morning to get their stretch on before they went about the rest of their day. Lucinda, Katie, Edgar, Maggie, and sometimes even Tyler; she'd made friends and she'd been welcomed into Laurel Cove just as she had hoped.

And to think, she'd almost gotten murdered and missed the opportunity.

Frank Tate, owner of Tate's Bussing, was in jail awaiting trial. His company faced innumerable lawsuits stemming from a bus accident that had been altogether preventable if not for his greed. Parker Frost was still recovering from his wounds but he had taken a plea deal. He had Lottie to thank in part for that. She'd told the prosecutor that, if not for Parker's whispered word *Romeo* she never would have known to tell Mae and her deputies where to search for the incriminating evidence.

The small notebook had been hidden in plain sight,

slipped between the pages of *Romeo and Juliet*, sitting on a shelf in Parker's office.

Lottie sprayed the yoga mats with cleaner and wiped them down. Once they were dry, she would roll them and stack them against the wall to be used again later for her afternoon Honey Flow class.

Cup of coffee in hand, Lottie watched the people as they passed by on Main Street going about their day. She heard the sirens before she saw the cars; two police cruisers flew by, lights flashing. Lottie glanced at her watch before setting her cup down on the window sill.

The next group weren't due at the studio for a while yet. She had time.

She pulled on her jacket, locked the door behind her, headed in the same direction that the Laurel Cove Sheriff's Department vehicles had gone.

She would keep her nose out of it this time. She'd promised. She *had* learned her lesson.

Lottie grinned. There was no harm in learning another one though … was there?

Marianne King

Marianne King grew up in Port-de-Grave, Newfoundland & Labrador and spent most of her life living in the province.

King's short story "Open the Door" was published in "Paper Mill Press" (2022), a creative arts journal produced annually from Grenfell Campus in Corner Brook, NL.

In March 2019, King won the Kit Sora Flash Photography Fiction contest with the story "The Perils of the Sea," and again in January 2023 with "Pinpoints of Light."

In 2024, her short story "Things Are Not What They Seem" was featured in *Cryptids from the Rock*.

Borrowing Trouble

There was a dead man in my library.

Morning light came through the stained-glass window, painting his bowed head and crisp suit in a geometric rainbow of blue, red, and yellow. His comfortable pose — slumped in a chair with an open book in his lap, giving the impression that he was reading — had made me pause when I'd arrived this morning. My first thought on seeing him had been to wonder how someone had gotten into the library. Beside him on a small low table was one of the library's pretty floral teacups, almost empty, and a half-eaten shortbread cookie on a matching plate. The citrusy scent of cold earl grey drifted through the room.

Sitting in front of him was Fitzy, his furry face staring in rapt bewilderment. The rainbows mixed with his tortoiseshell patterns, giving him a slightly psychedelic look. The cat was used to people being silent in the library, but it was the absolute stillness of the body that confused him.

"Fitzy," I whispered, holding my hand out and wiggling my fingers at him. He glanced in my direction, then ignored me, turning his head back to continue his observations. His paws hadn't moved. If I didn't find the scene so unnerving, I'd go over and pick him up, but I'd already checked the body for a pulse and I didn't want to get that close again.

A knock on the main door sounded, echoing in from the porch and I jumped, my hand going to my chest. When my pulse had slowed, I turned away from the reading area and walked to the front of the building. The main door of the library, a heavy wooden thing, squeaked as I pushed it open. It, along with the stained-glass windows, were the remnants and reminders of when the building was a church, and not a public library.

"Hi, Peter. Stacey." My voice sounded high to me, betraying how panicked I was. "I'm so glad you're here."

"Brynn," Officer Peter Peterson greeted me as he walked past into the building, followed by another officer, Stacey Chase. "Where's the body?"

I brought them to the sitting area, where Fitzy still sat, unmoved.

Officer Peterson observed the scene for a few moments, then turned to me and gently said, "The forensics team will be here shortly. Go home now, Brynn. Someone will be along later to question you." As he walked away, he called back, "And take your creepy cat with you, please!"

A few days later, gripping Fitzy's leash — walking was an activity his curious nature took great pleasure in, and the proximity of my house to the library enabled him to do it anytime weather permitted — I approached the library cautiously. As we weaved through the moss-covered headstones in the graveyard, yellow movement caught my eye, and I looked over to see a piece of caution tape caught on a windowsill, fluttering in the wind. Fitzy must have also spotted it, because he darted forward with a questioning, "Brrrrp?"

"No, Fitz," I muttered, scooping him up and holding him as we passed the window. "You are not playing with the caution tape."

The door swung open with a creak, the dim interior giving me pause. Taking a deep breath, I stepped inside, the faint smell of books and wooden furniture coming from inside the library calming me.

The porch extended to either side of me, longer than it was wide, with rods to hang coats running its length on each side of the front doors. While sometimes a patron hung their coat there, most preferred the security of keeping their coats with them. At each end of the long space was a washroom, one end for men and the other for women, but when the church became a library that changed, and now the washrooms were gender neutral. Straight ahead were the solid double doors to the library. One side stayed locked, and the other had a sign on it that said, *"DO NOT LET CAT OUT!"* in large, red block letters. Underneath, someone had written, *"No matter how nicely he begs"* with a black marker.

As I ran through my opening duties — emptying the dropbox, unlocking drawers, pulling any holds placed — and avoided looking toward the sitting area, my mind drifted back to the conversation I had had with Betty, my elderly next door neighbour, the previous day.

"His name was Greg Cobbett. He was staying at the

Bottom Bight Inn." Betty was sitting at my kitchen table, drinking tea and filling me in on all the gossip. Her perfectly curled hair and little old lady demeanor gave a Miss Marple-ish, trustworthy air, and she used this to her advantage. Everyone told her everything. "He attended high school here and from what I can recall and from speaking to people, he's not remembered with fond memories. Pretty much everyone I spoke to who either knew or encountered him had nothing nice to say at all."

I leaned against the counter, cupping my own mug in my hands. "I'm just glad that Fitzy doesn't like earl grey." The cat in question was curled up on the floor in a beam of sunshine when I looked in his direction.

Peter had been by the day before to see how I was doing, and to inform me that forensics was finished at the library. Before he'd left, he'd told me that after testing both the tea and shortbread, they'd found flunitrazepam — also known as the date rape drug — dissolved in the tea. A library pillow, which they'd taken as evidence, was then used to asphyxiate the victim. He confirmed with me that the tea, cup, and saucer had come from the library. I assured him that the shortbread hadn't, since I couldn't stand the stuff, so someone else must have brought it in from outside.

I filled Betty in on my conversation with him.

With all of my opening duties done, I settled behind the circulation desk to check my emails. A lot of them dealt with patron's inquiries about the death and, since I have a bad habit of signing up for newsletters, there were a few random library related emails in amongst them. Most of the newsletters were fluffy information pieces: children's programs, a lost parakeet spending the day in a supervisor's office, author visits. A few were a bit more serious: a devastating library fire, a rare book of birds stolen from a large city library, and hateful graffiti on a library building.

A light touch brushed my leg.

Chair wheels squealed as I pushed back from my desk with a shriek. Hand to my racing heart, I looked down.

"Mrrrow?"

Fitzy pranced out from under my desk, a look of feline joy on his face.

"Dammit, Fitzy!" I wiped at my leg where he had rubbed against it, glaring daggers as he strolled away, with not even a backward glance in my direction. Multicoloured tail held high, he headed into the reading area, presumably to his favourite cozy chair.

I rolled back to my desk, my concentration shattered. After staring at the screen for a few more minutes, I sighed and gave up. My mind just wasn't in the mood for work at the moment. Grabbing my cart of books, I headed for the shelves to put them away.

A knock at the library's main door brought my head around. As I walked through the porch, I could see Officer Peterson through the small, inset windows.

Peter and I had become good friends since I moved to Little Bottom Bight a few years back. His full name was Peter Peterson the Sixth. Out of curiosity, I'd asked him about his name once and he sheepishly informed me that calling the firstborn son Peter was a tradition in his family. Poor guy.

He was pulling out a notebook as I pushed the door

open.

"Morning, Brynn. Can I come in?"

I stepped back, swinging my arm to guide him to the interior doors. Once inside the library, he glanced at the book cart pushed halfway to the shelves, then back to me with a crooked smile. "Are you able to answer some questions?"

Looking pointedly at his notebook and pen, I responded, "Well, you've already got everything ready to go, so who am I to say no to the police?"

He blushed, then looked around hurriedly. "Well, is it better to go somewhere more comfortable," he swallowed audibly, "or would you prefer to answer questions here by the door?"

I smiled. "Why don't we move over to a table?" Best to get this over with, I thought.

Making sure that the sign said 'closed', I led him to the study area, where rows of tables waited for those in need of a quiet place.

We sat on opposite sides of a table near the circulation desk. I folded my hands in front of me and waited. He glanced around again, cleared his throat, then started.

He asked the expected questions: What was the victim doing in the library? The doors hadn't been forced, so how did they get in? Who else was in the library when I found the victim? Did I know the victim?

For the last question, he pulled out a photo and handed it to me. It was a picture of the victim, something most likely pulled off of a social media account. In it, the victim was smiling in the sunshine, palm trees in the background.

I answered with the expected replies. I don't know. I don't know, but they would need a key. There was no one else in the library that morning. I didn't know the…

A memory made me pause at the last question. I didn't know him, but I did remember him. He'd been in the library looking around a few days before I'd found his body.

"He was here, just a few days before in the afternoon," I whispered. My trembling hands made the photo shake. "Other than asking where specific sections were, he was just wandering around. Then he sat at a table and wrote in a notebook for a while. Numerous people were in the library that day asking questions, so I was in the shelves a lot. When I looked for him again, he was gone."

Peter's pen scratched across his paper. "And can you remember which sections he was interested in?"

"It was an assortment of topics." I leaned back in my chair and closed my eyes, trying to recall. "I remember him asking about mysteries, true crime, papermaking and bookbinding, old maps, and history books. There might have been more, but I can't remember." I shrugged.

Just then, Fitzy walked out of the stacks and headed for my desk chair, another favourite lounging spot in the library. I watched until I saw the chair spin slightly, its hydraulics squeaking, showing that he'd jumped up into it.

When I looked back at Peter, he was staring at his notebook, pen frozen.

Leaning over, I waved my hand over the notebook to get his attention. "Peter?"

He jumped, snapping his eyes up to mine. "I'm sorry, Brynn. I was just thinking." He wrote a few more things in his notebook, then stood up. "That'll be all for now, but I will ask if you could do two things for the police."

"Sure. What is it?"

"First, could you make a list of everyone that you remember was in the building during the time that he was here? We'll need to speak to them to see if they saw anything."

I nodded. "I'll try to remember."

"Second, so could you make a list of all the people who would have a key to the building? We need to start looking at suspects."

Nodding again, I got to my feet. "I'll work on it as soon as I can."

"Thank you. You've got my number, so if you think of anything else that would help the investigation, give me a call."

"I will."

"Then I'll let you get back to your work, Brynn. Have a good day." He turned, glanced around, and hurried out of the library.

I sat at the table a few minutes longer, wondering what had caused him to leave in such a rush. Finally, with a shake of my head and a muttered, "Back to work," I got up and walked over to my desk. As I approached my chair, Fitzy opened one eye and glared at me.

"Sorry, big guy, but I need my chair back." He didn't move. Instead, he rolled over and stretched, fully expecting some scratches on his exposed belly since it was a distraction tactic that had worked in the past.

I picked him up, cuddled him for a second, then placed him on the floor. "Not this time, Fitz. Something tells me it's gonna be a busy day."

And I was right.

As soon as I unlocked the door, patrons started filing in. Most of them, after a hurried, "Good morning" in my direction, headed for the side of the library to congregate in the sitting area, milling around the chairs and talking. They all, at some point or another, would get up the courage to approach me and ask about the murder and if the police had told me anything. I gave everyone the same story. "No, the police haven't told me anything more, and I'm sure they'll tell me if they feel I need to know." I hated to lie, but it kept gossip from spreading in the small town.

Fitzy had nestled himself comfortably in the reading area, jumping into the chair that I'd found the man in. From there he watched everyone, basking in the attention people gave him as they walked by. Whenever anyone asked which chair it was, I waved toward the general area, telling them it was the one by the coffee table. I couldn't bring myself to tell them it was the chair that they had just leaned over to scratch my cat's ears.

Other than the questions, I quickly discovered that most people didn't want to borrow anything, just gather and chat. I left them to it, finishing the shelving that Peter had interrupted that morning. Once I'd put all the books away, I sat in my chair and started on the two lists he'd requested.

There weren't many people who would have a library key, so I started with that list, since it wouldn't be a long one. I started with the obvious ones, including myself.

Librarian:
Brynn Murphy

Board -Members:
Chair — Sadie Chambers
Secretary — Henry Button
Treasurer — Alda Timmins

Town Hall:
Mayor — Bernard Bailey
Office Administrator — Cassie Regular
Head of Town Maintenance — Jerry Harnum

I stared at the screen, trying to think of anyone else who would have access to the library. At the moment, no names were coming to mind. Saving the document, I moved on to the list of people in the library the day that the victim had.

There had been lots of people in that day, so I wouldn't be able to remember them all, but I managed to recall a large percentage of them. Most had been in and out fairly quickly, but there had been a few that had stood out. Oddly enough, they were all on my library key list.

Alda, the board treasurer, had been here, happily telling me about a distant relative who would stay with her for a few weeks. This relative hadn't been to the town since they'd been a little girl.

Cassie, the office admin for the town hall, had also been in. After only a short amount of time, she'd come rushing out of an aisle with her books — a much smaller pile than usual — checking them out and leaving quickly.

I also remembered that Henry, the board secretary, had been in to ask me some questions about the upcoming meeting. He had been halfway through a sentence when he suddenly went very pale, then turned and left without saying goodbye.

Was there anyone else who had been in that afternoon acting strangely?

"Hi, Brynn!"

I jolted.

As if I had conjured her by doing up the lists, Alda stood at my desk. Her silver roots peeked out from her box-dyed red hair, conflicting with the beige sweater tucked into her high-waisted jeans, implying a youthfulness she wasn't ready to let go of yet. Beside her was an unfamiliar young woman, possibly in her late twenties, dressed in a simple white t-shirt and dark jeans. She was what most people would call "petite", made even more noticeable next to Alda's larger frame.

"Oh, hi, Alda! How are you today?"

"I'm just fine, Brynn! And yourself? Quite the goings on over the last few days." Alda looked around, taking in the crowd of people over by the chairs.

I looked over, too. "Let's just say it's been a busy morning."

"Oh, it looks like it. Such a shame. I remember teaching him at the high school." She slowly shook her head, her lips dropping into a sad frown.

"You taught him in high school?" I asked. "What was he like?"

"He wasn't easy to teach, but he was a good boy." Her eyes lost focus, thinking back and remembering.

The young woman picked a bookmark up from the circulation desk and Alda startled, putting a well-manicured hand to her mouth. "Oh, where are my manners?! Brynn, meet Abby Cavanagh, my cousin's daughter. She's the relative that I had mentioned would stay with me for a while."

I focused my gaze on the young woman. "Hi, Abby. How are you liking Little Bottom Bight so far?"

Abby, her dark hair pulled back in a low ponytail, was gazing around the library from where she stood, the bookmark forgotten in her hand. When I spoke to her, she gave a small jump, then smiled at me. "I'm loving it! It's just so quaint!"

Alda chuckled. "Yes, it's quite the small town compared to what Abby's used to. She grew up in Halifax, but she's also lived in much larger cities since then."

Another smile from Abby. "It seemed a lot bigger the last time I was here, but I was smaller then, so…"

"Yes, everything seems bigger when your memories are from your childhood." I returned the smile. "So, what are you ladies up to today? Are you showing Abby the sights, Alda?"

Alda's eyes sparkled. "Oh yes, indeed! We're going to go see the lighthouse and then have some fish and chips from that new takeout place."

A sudden hankering for some greasy food made me grin. "I hear they're absolutely delicious! You'll have to let me know."

"I will, Brynn. But," she shifted nervously on her feet. "I actually had another reason for coming in today, other than showing Abby the library. I was wondering if you could do me — well, us — a favour."

Alda usually wasn't the type to beat around the bush, so her hesitation was intriguing. "I will if I can. What do you need?"

"When I was telling Abby about the town, she got really excited when she heard about the library. It seems she's always loved books, and has been thinking of going back to school and doing library studies. Just to see how she likes it, I was wondering if she'd maybe be able to help you out sometimes." She looked fondly at Abby. "It'll also give her something to do while she's here."

I thought about it, all the tasks I could get her to do running through my mind. "I don't see why not." Smiling at Abby, I added, "Just give me a bit of time to figure out what I can get you to help me with. I'll call you tonight or tomorrow, Alda."

Alda bounced on her feet. "Oh, that'd be great, Brynn!"

"It's no problem. Now, why don't you show Abby around so that she gets a feel for the place."

They left, Alda chatting away. They headed through the seating area towards the children's area, petting down Fitzy as they passed.

The rest of the day went by quickly. Alda waved as she and Abby left, calling out a goodbye. After I locked up, Fitzy and I headed home. After making sure his water bowl was full, I grabbed my car keys and headed out to pick up some takeout, hoping to satisfy my earlier craving before meeting Betty for our walk.

Dusk was falling when Betty and I started on our walk. Stars twinkled in the darkening sky above us, fading as they got closer to the paler horizon.

Little Bottom Bight was a lovely town. Hugging the beach, where most of the businesses were, its roads meandered away from the water, full of colourful houses and buildings. There was one road that led to the provincial highway, and another that went along the coast, connecting it to other towns along the water. Our walks took us through the town and then down to the boardwalk that ran along the beach.

Betty was the first to break our silence. "So, how was your first day back?"

I chuckled. "Probably the busiest it's every been at that library."

Our nightly walk, and our friendship, had started just after I had moved to the Bight. I had been sitting on my porch swing, watching the sun set, when Betty had arrived on my steps, dressed in a pale pink jogging suit, a matching baseball cap flattening her silver curls.

She looked me up and down. "My doctor tells me I need to walk more," she said.

"Does he?" I continued to push the swing with my foot on the porch railing.

"You should join me."

My foot paused, the rhythmic creaking of the swing pausing with it. "Excuse me?"

Her face lit up with what I came to call her thousand-watt smile. "Well, I never like to stop talking for long, so I need company on my walks. And you seem lonely."

She'd been right.

We walked that night and every night we could after — a routine that cemented my most cherished friendship in the town.

The steady rhythm of our sneakers on the sidewalk was relaxing after my busy day. We walked in silence for a few minutes more.

Betty spoke up again. "Has Officer Peterson spoken to you again?"

"He was by first thing this morning, before I opened," I replied.

"Did he give you any more information about the investigation?"

"No. But — and keep this between you and me — he asked for a list of people who have keys to the library. I guess they're trying to figure out who has access after hours."

Betty was the town's unofficial information clerk. People told her everything, so she knew everything about everyone. But she also gave fantastic advice, so if you asked her not to repeat what you've told her, she wouldn't. I asked her about it once and she told me that if she went around blabbing everything everyone told her, no one would tell her anything.

Betty's eyes widened. "Really? And have you come up with a list of names yet?"

I watched my feet as I walked. "I have. As you can well imagine, it's not a long list, but longer than I thought it would be."

"Well, let's hear it, then."

So I went through the list with her. She nodded as she listened, commenting here and there, until I reached the town clerk, Cassie.

"An interesting story, there."

My feet stopped and I turned to her. "What do you mean?"

"Well, Cassie and your dead man were engaged. It was quite the scandal. The talk of the town."

"Engaged! When was this?" Then I paused, narrowing my eyes and giving her my best disapproving librarian face. "And he's not *my* dead man."

"Oh, it was about eight or nine years ago now. He left the poor girl standing at the altar." Sadness was in Betty's eyes. "Poor thing. It was the vows that did it. He decided he couldn't go through with it and just walked away from her, with a full church watching."

"That's awful!" My heart broke for Cassie, who was as sweet as could be.

"It was." Her pink clad shoulders lifted in a shrug. "I've heard that she's never really gotten over it, which is why she's alone. She was never able to trust anyone with her heart again."

"Poor Cassie!" I started walking again, and heard Betty's feet slapping on the sidewalk behind me, a splash of pink in the corner of my eye as she caught up.

Betty nodded. "I know. Hopefully, she'll learn to trust again at some point." Scuffing her feet, she put her head down and murmured, "But, just how upset is she?"

Glancing over at her, I asked, "What do you mean?"

"Well, is she upset enough to seek revenge?"

"Betty!" I gasped. "That's an awful thing to say about

Cassie!"

Again, Betty shrugged. "True, but is it unbelievable? If someone had broken your heart and your trust, not to mention having at least half the town witness your humiliation, how far would you go if you wanted revenge?"

I really thought about it. "I have to say that I truly don't know. I've never had my heart broken badly enough to even think about it."

"While we think we know people on the outside, we never truly know what they're capable of on the inside," Betty replied.

"This is true."

Betty stopped under a streetlight, the orange glow turning her walking suit into a ghastly coral colour. "And with that, dear Brynn, our walking and talking are done for the day."

I looked up at my car in the driveway, realizing that night had completely fallen while we'd walked and talked and we were back on our street. Blinking, I turned back to Betty. "Our walk's over already?"

Her smile went up a few watts. "Time flies when you're having fun, Brynn! I'll see you tomorrow." Then she walked to her own driveway.

Waving at her back, I wished her a good evening. My stairs creaked as I walked up them, moths fluttering around my porch light.

Fitzy greeted me as I opened the door, then pivoted and walked away toward the kitchen, tail held high. He paused at the entrance to glance back at me. Obviously, it was treat time.

"Just give me one minute, Fitzy. I've got to do something first." Heading for my office, I flicked on the light and sat at my desk, booting up my laptop.

After I had finished my list of people with access to the library key today, I'd forwarded it on to Officer Peterson, then I sent another copy to myself. Opening the document, I highlighted Cassie's name, then put an asterisk next to it. Beside her name, I wrote *'left at the altar by victim'*.

The clatter of a bowl being flung across a linoleum floor, accompanied by a loud disgruntled meow, sounded from the kitchen.

"All right, all right! I'm coming!" I called out.

Standing, I took another look at the list, wondering if there were any others on the list who had connections with Greg Cobbett. Connections that they might kill for.

I might have to dig a little deeper into the people on my list.

"I have some possibly relevant information for you."

As always, Betty didn't knock. She came in the back door, made herself some tea, then settled herself at my kitchen table before she spoke. It had been two days since we'd talked about Cassie. I'd already told Peter about our conversation.

I quirked an eyebrow at her. "Do tell," I said, then went back to flipping my eggs.

Her face was solemn. "It's about Henry Button."

My spatula paused above the pan, an egg balanced precariously on it. "As in, library board Henry?" The egg sizzled as I put it back in.

"That's the one."

Grabbing a plate from the cupboard, I placed my eggs on it, then turned to her and gestured at the egg carton beside me, silently asking if she'd like some. She shook her head, declining. "And what is this gossip you have on poor Henry?"

Betty took a sip of her tea. "It's not gossip. I was thinking about who would want to kill Greg, and I recalled he bullied Henry mercilessly at school. I remember it got pretty bad."

With a loud, springy sound, my toast slices popped up. I quickly buttered them, the scrape of the knife loud in the kitchen, then set them next to my eggs.

The utensils in my top drawer clattered as I pulled out a fork. Pulling out a chair from the table, I sat down across from Betty.

Henry was a quiet man. He'd been the library board secretary for years now, since before I'd started working there. Always well-dressed, with thick-rimmed glasses and a serious face. His soft voice and competent demeanor made you want to trust him.

I tried to think of what he would have been like in high school. Easily, I could picture him as an irresistible target for bullies.

"Would you like to know how bad it got?"

Betty's quietly serious question broke me from my thoughts. I focused on her, then nodded.

"Most of it was the usual stuff. Name calling, knocking his books out of his hands, tripping him up. I remember him as a teen. He was all angles and clumsiness." She sighed. One of those really deep sighs that comes from wherever sadness is hiding inside. I knew she was fond of Henry. He brought out a streak of protectiveness in his friends.

"What did Greg do to him?"

Her eyes focused on me. "It was while everyone was getting changed after gym class. He took pictures of Henry and posted them all over the school. Poor boy! He never got over it." Her hands wrapped around her teacup, warming her up. "The ridicule got so bad that he ended up quitting school. Had to do his GED to get his diploma. He never wanted to stay here after that."

"What do you mean?"

"He was going to move away from here once he got his GED. Didn't stop talking about it."

I leaned forward. "So why didn't he? What happened?"

Betty gave a sad smile. "His mom got sick, and he stayed. She passed away a few years after that, but he never left." She fiddled with the spoon she had used for her tea. "Can you imagine? Living in a town that you hated, that never lets you forget the most embarrassing time of your life? And then one day, the person who caused it all shows up again." The last part wasn't a question, it was a statement.

"So, you think Henry could have killed him?"

"I don't know. But it's definitely a possibility."

Betty left shortly after that. She'd told me what she wanted to, so she left me to ponder what she'd said. After she left, I went to my office and pulled up my list again. Beside Henry's name, I wrote *'bullied by victim in high school'*.

This meant I had two suspects with access to the key and a motive. Cassie and Henry. How many more people with unhappy connections to Greg Cobbett were on my list?

It also meant I had another name to give to Peter.

Dust motes were shimmering in multi-coloured sun-beams, and Fitzy was dancing after them, jumping up to grab at the air.

It was a slow afternoon. Abby had come and gone, and there was a lull, with no patrons at all in the building.

Abby had been by every day since Alda had asked me if she could help. At first, I'd given her small chores to do around the library, like dusting the shelves and picking up any books that patrons had left on the tables or in the sitting area. When those tasks were done, I would find her wandering amongst the shelves, looking at the books and familiarizing herself with our classification system. Once I knew she was serious about her interest in library work, I gave her tasks that were a bit more interesting, like help-ing a patron find a book or shelving the returns, which she particularly seemed to enjoy.

Off and on all day, I'd been thinking about Henry and his awful experience in high school. Since it was quiet, I decided it was the perfect time to pull out the school year-books and see if I could find him in there.

The library's back room held the yearbooks. I placed my tap bell on my desk, along with the 'Ring bell for ser-vice' sign, just in case anyone came in while I was back there. As I headed back, Fitzy joined me, his tail an inquisitive question mark.

Fitzy loved the back room. There were so many boxes and shelves to inspect, along with places to hide. Whenever he followed me back there, I had to inspect the room before I left. I'd also gotten into the habit of keeping a container of treats by the door, which I shook every time I left the room, just in case he'd gotten in when I wasn't looking.

Crossing through the children's area, I opened the door and he trotted in, throwing me a happy trill as he went. He quickly tucked himself behind some boxes, a shuffling sound indicating which direction he was heading.

The back room wasn't big, but there was a lot of stuff in there. Shelving units full of books and boxes lined the walls. There was everything from an old set of encyclopedias to program supplies. In the middle of the room was a small table with some chairs placed around it.

I located the yearbooks, found the years I was looking for, and brought them back to the table. Opening the earliest of the three years, I paged through to the B's, looking for Henry's picture and finding it. He looked bright and happy in this first image, full of excitement for the coming year. In the second yearbook, his smile had dimmed a little. This was the year that he'd gotten his glasses. When I got to his final year of high school, his smile was gone completely and he looked thinner, sadder.

My heart broke for him, but at the same time, I wondered if this was the high school face of a killer.

Thunk.

The sound of something hitting the floor startled me.

I stood up, turning to the sound. Fitzy sat on a shelf at chest level, looking proud of himself. On the floor below was an opened box, turned on its side, with its contents spilling out.

"Fitzwilliam Darcy! What do you think you're doing?"

For a second, he almost looked sheepish, but then he remembered he was proud of his newest accomplishment.

I crouched and righted the box, then started stuffing everything back in. Surprisingly, there wasn't much. Just some blankets and a book. Since I don't normally store the backroom books in boxes, I picked it up.

It was a large, thick book, with an engraved and gilded bird on the cover. It looked old, very old. I carefully opened it, wincing at the crackling sound the spine made. I looked at a few of the pages, unable to stop myself from running my fingers over their smoothness. They had beautiful, colourful images of birds, with the name and description of each below it. The Florida Cormorant, the Ring-Necked Duck, and the Oregon Snow Bird were a few of the birds that I spotted. As I turned the pages, I could feel how thin they were and I worried I might damage them.

I'd never seen this book before.

Where had it come from?

As I stared at the book, confused, a small article in a library newsletter that I'd read recently came to mind. It had mentioned a rare book about birds being stolen from a library. Putting the box back on the shelf — Fitzy had moved on by now — I took the book out to the circulation desk. Pulling up my email, I searched for the newsletter, opening it when I found it and staring at the picture included.

It was the same book.

I'd found the stolen book. Here. In my library.

After staring at it on my desk for a few minutes more, I did the only thing that made sense. I called Peter.

When Peter and Stacey arrived, I put a sign on the front door saying I'd be back in fifteen minutes and closed the library. Placing the book on a table, we all sat around and looked at it for a few seconds.

Stacey spoke first. "So, you think this book is stolen?"

"I'm one hundred percent certain that it is." Before they'd arrived, I'd printed up the newsletter article to give to them. I placed it on the table and pushed it to her.

She picked it up and read it, compared the image to the book on the table, then handed the sheet to Peter. He repeated her actions, then laid the sheet down in front of him. He then pulled the book over and started leafing through it.

I tensed, anxious about the book's fragility. "Please be careful," I said. "It's old."

He paused and glanced up at me, then slowly closed the cover. "Why would this book be here?" he asked.

Putting my elbows on the table, I shrugged. "I have no idea." I rubbed my face as I pondered the question, then paused when a thought hit me. "We have a dead man and a stolen rare book, both found in the same library, in the same week. Do you think it's a coincidence?"

Peter shook his head. "I don't know." Picking up the article again, he skimmed through it. "This book was stolen from the same city that Greg Cobbett was living in before he came here." He glanced up at me. "Would you happen to have any idea how much a book like this would go for if auctioned?"

"I do." While I'd waited for them, I'd researched the book. "As far as I can tell, there aren't that many copies of this edition. People have paid over a million dollars for them."

Peter gave an impressed whistle. "That's a lot for an old bird book. With that amount of money and the timeline, I think there's a very likely connection between these two crimes. The victim is quite possibly our thief." He stood and picked up the book. Stacey stood up with him.

"We'll take the book with us and keep it at the station until we're done with our inquiries." Turning, they walked away, then looked back after a few steps. "Thanks for finding this, Brynn. It might be a clue."

"Oh, don't thank me." I waved toward the sitting area, where Fitzy was curled up in a chair, watching us. "Thank Fitzy. He's the one who found it."

He looked over, then stiffened, giving a shaky smile. "You can thank him for me." Turning, he left the library, Stacey close behind.

I stared after them, then over at Fitzy. "He sure gets jumpy when Fitzy's around," I muttered to myself, then went out in to the porch and unlocked the door.

The rest of the afternoon passed quietly, and when Cassie, the town clerk, came in thirty minutes before closing, it surprised me. She hadn't been to the library since the day Greg had been here looking for some items.

Cassie seemed nervous as she wandered the shelves, and I noticed she kept glancing toward the chairs.

There was nobody else in the building, and churches were designed to have fantastic acoustics, so she heard me clearly when I softly asked, "You knew him, didn't you?"

She paused, the book she was pulling down tilting on the shelf's edge, then she pushed it back in as she put her head down, her straight blond hair covering her face. Picking up the books she'd already collected, she came up to the desk, placing the books and her library card on it.

"Yes, I knew him." There wasn't a hint of sadness in her voice or her face. "I'm sure you've already heard that he left me at the altar." She waved toward the children's area. "Specifically, this altar."

I blinked. "The ceremony was here?" I put her at the top of my very short list of possible killers.

"It was. He listened to me tearfully say my vows to him, and then when it was his turn, all he could say was 'I'm sorry, I just can't'. And then he walked down the aisle and out the doors of an absolutely quiet church." Her lips twisted in a wry smile. "Truthfully, it was the best thing that could have happened."

I blinked again. "It was?" I couldn't hide the shock in my voice.

"Of course it was! Can you imagine being married to him?" She shuddered.

"What was he like?" My voice was quiet when I asked.

"He was incredibly mean, and incredibly selfish." Her eyes were clear when she said it, focused on me. "People had told me what he was like, but I didn't want to believe them. Looking back now, the signs were there, but I was too young and stupid to see them." She shook her head. "I hated him, but I didn't want him dead. If anything, I would have thanked him if I'd seen him again."

I recalled my conversation with Alda. "It's funny. Most people have nothing nice to say about him, except for Alda. According to her, he was hard to teach, but a good kid."

Cassie snorted out a laugh. "Alda said that?"

Nodding, I replied, "Almost word for word."

She shook her head. "Greg treated Alda like garbage in high school. He was always rude, calling her cruel names and playing pranks on her. She was the teacher he picked on the most, embarrassing her almost every day. If anything, I doubt she truly thinks that he was a good kid." She pushed her books towards me with a smile and continued, "Now, please scan my books so that we can both go home."

"I know how we can find the book thief, and if they're connected, the killer."

It was later that night. I'd gotten home from work and instantly headed to my computer to update my list. After crossing out Cassie's name, I added *'victim was cruel to her when she taught him in high school'* next to Alda's.

I was eating my supper, a very bland, microwaved meatloaf dinner, when Peter called, blurting out his thought without even saying hello.

"What do you mean?" I asked.

"Well, I was thinking, if it's all right with you," here he paused, then continued, "that maybe we could spread a rumour that the book is hidden in the library's back room. Then, for the next few nights, we could have some officers hiding in the library, waiting to see if anyone comes sniffing around."

I thought about it. It was a good plan, but what if the book thief found out that it was a trap? I voiced this to Peter.

"The worst that could happen is that they don't show up," he replied.

This was true.

"Normally, we'd have to run this by the board, but in this situation, I don't think that's a good idea." I told him what I'd found out about Alda.

"That's interesting. I'll have to look into it. But you're right," he agreed. "For now we'll have to keep the board in the dark."

We talked some more, working out a plan of action. We decided I would let the police in through the side door right before I closed up, then I would leave. I gave him some bits of advice, including the best places that the police could hide.

We had a solid plan, but Peter was concerned with one thing: "Who should we get to spread the rumour?"

I grinned, despite knowing that he couldn't see it. "Don't you worry about that, Peter. I've got just the person."

The next night, I went through all of my closing duties and then I let the police in through the side door and left.

In the morning, Peter called to inform me that no one had shown up.

For a week, this went on. Each night, the police would

arrive at the library's side door every evening just before closing. I'd let them in and lock up the library, and then go home where I anxiously waited, not able to sleep.

Betty assured me she was subtly spreading the word of the book's location, so she couldn't understand why nothing was happening. "I don't understand," she kept telling me. "I've told every single busybody I know, making them promise not to tell anyone. There's no way they're not blabbing all over town after making that sort of promise. They just can't help themselves."

I assured her they had been blabbing. I'd overheard conversations throughout the town about the book. As Betty said, people just couldn't help themselves.

Finally, the police had given up.

"I'm sorry, Brynn. Nothing seems to happen, and we just can't afford to keep paying the extra personnel to stay at the library every night." Peter was apologetic as he told me this. I worried about being alone, but I knew they couldn't keep coming back every night to wait for something that might not happen. It looked like the killer had moved on, giving up on their prize.

Over the next few days, I slowly got back into my routine. Get up, go to work, go home. No waiting for the police every evening.

On the fourth evening, Fitzy and I had just gotten home when I realized I'd left my cell phone at the library.

"Shit!" I pulled my empty hand out of my pocket, where my phone was supposed to be. Closing my eyes in exasperation, I pictured it by the landline on the circulation desk, where I'd placed it so I wouldn't forget.

Apologizing, I removed Fitzy's harness and hung it

up. "I've gotta go back, buddy. You know I'm lost when I don't have my phone."

His furry face looked at me hopefully as I backed up to the door, and he took a step toward me, then looked at his harness.

"I'm sorry, Fitzy. I really am." I hated leaving him, but taking him would stretch the time twice as long because he loved to stop and investigate everything.

It was one of those beautiful fall evenings, where everything seemed crisp and the moon tried to hide behind sparse clouds. The walk back to the library was calming, and I was feeling rejuvenated as I let myself into the building.

The foyer was dark, but I didn't bother turning on any lights. I'd be in and out quickly. The inside

door opened with a quiet shush across the floor, and as it closed, the humming of the exit signs was all I could hear, the stillness of the library enveloping me. Using the light from the street, I navigated my way to the circulation desk.

My phone was right where I'd left it.

Thump.

I froze, my hand reaching out to the desk, and looked toward the back of the building.

"Hello?" My voice echoed in the quiet, but there was no response. I strained my ears, listening, but there were no other sounds.

Picking up my phone, I dialed Peter, thankful that years of working in a library formed a habit of keeping my phone on silent. I turned the volume down as low as it would go and, knowing I would still hear him, I covered the speaker with my thumb. I listened for the phone to ring, holding it to my ear, and when I heard him answer, I quietly and slowly walked toward the back of the library.

One good thing about being very familiar with a space is that if you need to walk around in the dark, you can.

"Hello? Is there someone in the library?" I called again, mostly for the benefit of Peter, letting him know where I was.

It got darker the further back I went. The back of the library faced away from the street, so the light faded as I got further past the rows of shelving. By the time I reached the children's area, the only light was the eerie red glow from the exit sign above the side door.

Pausing, I listened again, hoping to hear something. To my left was the newspaper and microfilm room, its door shut. On the other side of the children's area, I could barely see the door to the back room. From where I was, I couldn't see if it was open or closed.

I crept toward it, hoping that my steps weren't as loud as they sounded to my ears. As I got closer, I could see that the door was open a bit, though I had locked it earlier. I slowed, then stopped outside the door, gathering my courage.

Stepping forward, I pushed open the door and, knowing exactly where the light switch was, flicked it on and peered inside. Momentarily blinded, I blinked until my vision cleared.

"Abby?"

She stood with her back to the shelves, a box hugged to her stomach. I got the impression that she'd been trying to stay as still as possible. At first, she looked shocked, but then her face hardened. She turned, placing the box on the shelf behind her, then turned back. "What are you doing here, Brynn? You were supposed to be gone home for the night."

"What am *I* doing here? What are *you* doing here?" I stepped further into the room, looking around at the chaos she'd created. There were empty boxes everywhere, their contents spilled out. Papers and books littered the floor. "How did you even get in?"

Abby stepped toward me. "Where is it?"

"Where's what, Abby?" I knew what she was looking for, but I feigned confusion. I hoped Peter could hear my conversation.

"Where's the book?"

"You'll have to be more specific, Abby. We're surrounded by books." I put my hand out — the one not holding my phone — and gestured around the room.

"The book about birds! I know it's here! I've been hearing *whispers*," she brought her hands up and jerked her fingers in 'air quotes', "for a few weeks now!" Her face, which had seemed hard until now, twisted in frantic anger.

I realized I was in the room with a possible killer.

"The bird book?" I tried to keep my voice steady. "You mean the rare book that was stolen? Is that what this is all about?" I slowly took a step back toward the open door.

"YES!" She threw her arms up and spun around, then stopped, facing me. "Do you know how long it took to steal that thing?! All the planning and the convincing. And then *he* had to ruin it!"

"He?" Another step back. "Do you mean Greg Cobbett?"

"Yes! I was supposed to meet him here in this stupid town so that he could give me the book, but he hid it from me." She was pacing, kicking her way through the mess on the floor.

"What did you do, Abby?" Was the door close enough?

She went still, her eyes narrowing. Her gaze flicked down to the phone in my hand.

"Who's on the phone, Brynn?" Her voice was soft, menacing.

I hadn't noticed that her kicking and pacing had brought her closer to me. I spun, then ran. The blackness of the library enveloped me, my eyes still adjusted for light. I could hear her scrambling after me, yelling. I had hoped the mess she'd created would slow her down, but she was already running freely, outside the room and chasing me.

With my hands extended in front of me, I ran through the children's area, then leaped down the stairs into the sitting area. Could I make it to the main light switch? My finger had moved off of the phone speaker, and I could hear Peter's muffled voice yelling my name.

The tables and chairs were a gauntlet, but I navigated them quickly. Abby's steps were close behind me. The light switches were just ahead, to the left of the inner doors.

My hand was reaching for the switch when Abby caught my sweater and pulled me back, throwing me to the floor.

"I asked who was on the phone, Brynn." She stood over me, a menacing shadow.

I braced myself on my elbows, trying to sit up, as the room lit up with flashes of blue and red, and sirens wailed.

Abby looked toward the windows.

The police had arrived.

"It's Officer Peterson. That's who's on the phone." She looked back at me as I held up my phone up, the call screen visible.

From outside, car doors slammed and a tinny voice echoed through a megaphone. "Abby Cavanagh , this is the police."

Her eyes widened, then darted to the window again. "You called the police?" she whispered.

Though she didn't see it, I nodded. "I called the police. It's over, Abby."

"No, it's not." Then she took off running, heading for the back of the library again.

"Abby!" I yelled after her. "Where are you going?" Scrambling to my feet, I followed her. I was close enough to see her hit the push bar on the side door and hear the creak as it swung open. She raced through the door, and I heard a muffled "Oof". Abby reappeared again, being pushed through the door by Peter. He handcuffed her, reading her rights as she struggled.

Then he saw me. "Brynn! Are you okay?"

I nodded, then turned and stumbled back to the light switches, with Peter following me, pulling Abby along with him as he walked. The library illuminated, dimming the flashing lights from outside.

When he reached the main doors, he contacted the police outside, then led Abby out to a waiting police car. Once she was seated in the back of the cruiser, he returned to check on me, then asked me if I was up to answering some questions at the station.

It was at the station that the adrenaline wore off. I gave a report of the what happened, then they sent me home.

Fitzy greeted me at the door with a disgusted look for leaving him, then walked away.

I stumbled to my bedroom and dropped facedown across the bed fully clothed. Pyjamas required energy. The bed dipped as Fitzy jumped up, then curled in beside me. I put my arm around him, his fur soft against my skin, and was asleep in seconds.

"So the whole thing was her idea?"

Peter and I sat at a small corner table at the local café, surrounded by the murmuring crowd and the scent of caffeine and baked goods. The small café was a popular spot for tourists, especially when there was a chill in the air, so we were lucky to have snagged a table.

He placed his mug on the rickety table, swallowing his mouthful of coffee before he replied. "It was. She had found out about the book from the library's website. Deciding on the long game, she planned it all, from acquainting herself with Greg so that he could take the fall, to convincing him to steal the book. Even hiding it here in Little Bottom Bight. He did everything, and then he got suspicious and came to the town before her, hiding the book in the library."

Which is why he was in the library that day, asking about different topics. "And she confessed to it all?" Feeling chilled, I wrapped my hands around my mug, letting the warmth seep into my fingers.

"Yep. Everything from the planning, to the stealing, to

the killing."

I slumped back into my chair. "Poor Alda has to be devastated. She was so excited about Abby coming to visit."

"She blames herself. Yesterday she came in to give a statement, telling us everything she knew, which wasn't much. Abby completely pulled the wool over her eyes." His own eyes were sad, and I remembered that his mother and Alda were close friends.

I nodded, looking out at the grey waves crashing on the beach. The well-insulated window kept me from hearing the rocks clicking with the rushing in and out of the water, but I really wished I could. It was such a calming sound. "It'll take time, but the hurt will fade."

"Yes, it will," he replied.

If I hadn't been looking back at him as he spoke, I would have missed it, but just as he finished, a notification chimed over the crowd from somewhere in the room. It was a very realistic sound of an alarmed cat and he stiffened, eyes going wide in fear, his pupils dilating.

And I finally figured it out, all the clues coming together.

"You're afraid of cats!" For some reason, this delighted me. How had I not noticed before? He was a police officer. Weren't they supposed to be rescue cats from trees?

His cheeks flushed pink and he dipped his chin, looking down at his empty mug. His knuckles whitened on the handle. "I was wondering if you'd realize," he mumbled.

"Why didn't you say something? I could have made sure that Fitzy wasn't around when you were."

He gave a small sigh. "Because it's a silly fear. A cat

clawed me up badly years ago, and I always worry that it'll happen again. Every time I'm close to one, I get pan-icked."

"Everyone's afraid of something, so it's not a silly fear. No fear ever is." I smiled at him. "If you'd like, you can hang around with Fitzy at the library and see if you can get used to him. He's pretty chill, even with kids."

His face quickly matched his knuckles.

I put my hands up, palms out toward him. "Or, we can forget I ever mentioned it!"

He was quiet for a moment, the conversations around us filling in the silence, then he looked at me. "Maybe."

"Maybe?"

He gave me a small, lopsided smile. "Baby steps."

I extended my hand over the table. "Shake on it."

He stared, then asked, "Really?"

"Shaking on baby steps." My hand remained over the table.

Sighing, he shook. "It's still maybe."

I agreed. "Still maybe."

My chair creaked as I leaned back from the table. I looked around at the busy café, then back at Peter. "I guess things are going to slow down in Little Bottom Bight again, aren't they?"

"Oh, I don't know about that. After all," he grinned, "you seem to have a knack for borrowing trouble."

Chelsea Bee

Chelsea Bee is a bestselling author from Arnold's Cove, Newfoundland.

She has a Bachelor of Arts, a Diploma in Creative Writing, and a Certificate of Criminology from Memorial University. She is currently a Masters student at the University of Surrey, and is residing in Guildford, England, with her very noisy calico cat.

Since 2017 she has written three novels, *London Calling*, *Christmas Mornings*, and *Fall with Me*.

A Death in Dover

I take the wooden mallet and slam it down on the top of the cask of beer. This is the first one I've had to tap today, and so far, this one hasn't given me any trouble. They've been sitting on the rack behind the bar for a week now, so they've mostly settled.

About six months ago I started running my dad's pub. It's technically not a pub; it was always an alehouse. He loved the real ales, and since we're able to get so many of them locally, he decided to tap into that market. It was an old cobbler's shop before my dad bought it when I was a little kid. It was always a bright red beacon on the top of the old high street. There were a number of alehouses in town at the time, but they've all since closed, leaving Henderson's the only one in Dover. There are a couple of other alehouses in the rest of Kent, and we spent many weekends of my childhood visiting them.

In the past decade, Dad finally relented and put a couple of beer taps on the bar as well as introducing spirits and a cocktail menu. The times were changing, and the strict ale drinkers were getting fewer and far between. Dad always made sure, though, that the beers on tap were craft or European beers. He didn't want anything in his alehouse that you could also find in a bottle at Sainsbury's. So, eventually we evolved fromm an alehouse to a pub, but remained the same family friendly gathering place he always wanted it to be.

I tap the second cask and jump away just in time before the amber liquid fizzles and hits the wall. Sometimes they get shaken up a bit more in transit and they're livelier when we do tap them. They have to wait on the rack for at least a week or half of the beer would end up on the floor. But we ran out of most of our ales last night, so I have no choice but to open these a little earlier than I'd like.

At quarter past noon, my coworker, Gareth, strides through the front door, the bell chiming behind him. He normally arrives at exactly opening time, but today he's slightly late.

"I was beginning to doubt you'd make an appearance," I say.

"You alright, Gemma. What a job getting out of the bloody house," he greets me in a thick Northern accent. He spent ten years in the army after finishing up school in Yorkshire. Once he left, he went on a road trip down the coastline and eventually settled in Kent, trying to find a place to spend a couple of weeks for a holiday. He ended up meeting his wife, who was a local, and never left. He started working for my dad about eight years ago, helping him run the pub when Dad couldn't. At the time I was living in London. I could barely get home, even though the train ride is a quick hour until I got back. But I spent nearly every day of the week in my small cubicle of my magic circle law firm office.

Once I got the call that Dad had a stroke, I quit my job and packed up my small flat and took the train home.

I had a couple more weeks with Dad. But I knew that he would have wanted me to keep the pub running. And honestly, in the ten years I worked as a solicitor, I hated it. I had a decent salary that all went toward basic living expenses, and I never had the time to enjoy living in London. By the time I left, I think most tourists on a one-week stay had seen more of the city than I did. When I left the city, I moved into his small cottage, which meant I also inherited his border collie, Lady. She spends the day with me in a corner of the pub reserved for her.

I tap the third keg. This time, a dark liquid pours from the top like a volcano, soaking me in milk stout.

"Blimey," Gareth laughs, his arms crossed in front of him.

"This is so not funny! I need to go home; I'm soaked," I say. Not to mention, there's real milk in the milk stout. It's a chilly autumn morning, so we have the fireplace on. If I stay here for much longer, I'm going to smell like sour milk.

"You go on home, we're not going to be overrun with customers at noon on a Wednesday," Gareth says, opening a package of pork scratching and popping one into his mouth. At the smell of the bag opening, Lady immediately pops her head up to see if one of them are on offer. They're not, they're far too crunchy for her old lady teeth.

"I'll leave Lady here, you'll be fine. I just need to go quickly. I'll be back in an hour, tops," I say and grab my front door key and my messenger bag.

Normally I take the bus to work; Dover is so hilly, my

legs would be aching by the time I get home. But I don't want to get on the bus with a soaked shirt and smelling of beer in the middle of the workday, so I take the footpath across town to get home.

The footpath is long, until it eventually opens up to a sunflower field, and my cottage is not far from there. Halfway through the path, I see something blocking it in the distance blocking the way.

Strange, but not unheard of. Probably a bike that someone left abandoned, or some garbage left by fly tippers.

I walk up closer to the item and quickly realize it's not a thing. It's a *person*.

I jog up to the man lying on his side and laying across the path. His eyes are closed, and he looks like he's been here for some time. It's a chilly morning, and it looks like there's no warmth left in his body. I can't see much of him, but I know his condition isn't good.

I take my phone out and immediately call 999.

I take a couple of steps back and wait for the police to arrive. They said I don't need to wait with him, since there are no signs of life, but I can't leave a man all alone on the road.

It doesn't take long before Officer Wilson arrives. He's the chief of police for the local area. He's been a regular at Henderson's since I can remember. I assumed he would be the one here, as crimes like this don't happen here often. It's a small town, though it's gotten more populated over recent years as work from home was introduced and people started moving into the countryside from London. But for the most part, the locals all know each other.

"Afternoon, Gemma," Officer Wilson says.

"Hi, Brian," I say and give him a small wave.

"Thanks for staying with him," he says.

"Do you know who it is?" I ask. There's a paramedic carrying a gurney down the long footpath and approaching us. I see him get loaded onto the gurney. I look away, it feels wrong to see him in a vulnerable position.

"Yeah, don't you recognize him?" he asks. "It's Carl; he was a regular at Henderson's. Captain of the darts team."

And then it dawns on me. Of course he was. I should have recognized him from his long beard and bushy eyebrows. Though he was slumped over and on his side, and I didn't want to touch him, so I didn't really see his face.

Why would anyone want to hurt a nice old man?

I didn't know Carl well, but he was always nice. He never overdid it on the ales and never got into fights outside the pub, which is more than I can say for most of our customers. Even the nicest of people can be rowdy after they've had one too many.

"How long do you think he was out here?" I ask.

"I won't be able to tell," Officer Wilson says. "It looks like he met the wrong person on the path… It can't have been recent, though. Maybe some time last night."

"Would anyone have seen him?" I ask and look around, as if expecting a witness to come forward. Truth is, I don't know how many people would take this path at night.

"Don't worry about it, we'll take care of it and do a full investigation," he says, and walks past me to talk to the paramedic.

I want to stay and ask questions. What did he mean

by 'met the wrong person'? Surely no one in Dover is looking to hurt anyone else, right? Granted, I don't think he would have been bleeding if it was from natural consequences. The only wildlife around here are foxes, and they normally aren't seen in this area. The path is right next to a commercial area so it's pretty busy, even late at night. I almost never see a fox here.

I watch as they load Carl into the ambulance, knowing there's nothing I can do to help him. I accept defeat and continue on the path home.

I feel slightly unsettled taking the path that that Carl just died on, but I still have to get home and get changed.

I quickly walk past the area Carl's body was found. A chill goes down my spine. I have no idea where the person who killed him was — what if it was a local? I have no idea if it was a targeted attack or random. I can only assume it was targeted. No one but locals use this path, and whoever did it had to know his routine and know the area well.

I get home and quickly change my shirt, putting the old one in the washing machine and turning it on.

I quickly get back to work, my thoughts with Carl the entire walk home

I get back to Henderson's as quickly as possible.

"How was your walk?" Gareth asks.

"Absolutely awful," I say and drop my messenger bag on the floor behind the bar.

"What happened?" he asks. He finishes pouring the beer and hands it across the bar to Ollie. He's a regular customer who is on Henderson's darts team with his dad. He's been coming here since we were both kids. His parents used to come to Henderson's every weekend, and they'd bring Ollie in tow. I was always here because I didn't have a babysitter. We went to different schools — he went to the boy's school and I went to the school for girls — but we always spent time together. To be honest, I had a bit of a crush on him in our teenage years.

"You know Carl, right? I found him dead on the footpath that cuts across town," I say, still in shock slightly.

"Carl Brown?" Ollie asks incredulously.

I just nod in response.

"Oh, no," he says, pulling up a barstool and sitting down.

"Were you close?" Gareth asks.

"No, I guess not," Ollie says. "It's just that I've known him for years. He went to school with Dad back when they were kids. So they weren't close friends, but they knew each other well enough. And I joined the darts team when I was, what...sixteen maybe? It was before I could even drink. Anyway, I've just known him for the better part of a decade. I'm just in a bit of a shock."

"Do you know anyone who would have wanted to hurt him?" I ask.

"I'm not sure. We'll have to do some asking around town," he says.

"Are you sure you want to start sniffing around a murder investigation?" Gareth asks. He takes a long drink of his water. He looks nervous; he must be afraid to walk home after work after what happened to Carl.

"Yeah, I think I have to. What if it's someone local?" I ask.

"I'm sure the police will be investigating," Gareth

says.

"They're busy. I know they'll investigate, but there will be other cases as well. You and I both use the footpath to get home, I really don't want to walk there at night knowing that something could happen."

"At least you have Lady," Gareth says, looking over at my dog asleep on the blanket in front of the fireplace.

"She's never had to protect me before, I don't know what her reaction would be. She's friendly, so what if she's too friendly? I don't want to risk it and find out," I say.

"Sorry, Gemma, do you think you can hold down the fort for today?" Gareth asks, "I don't really feel well."

"Yes, of course. What's wrong? You seemed fine this morning," I say. A couple of customers start to filter in as the late afternoon approaches and some people come in for a drink after finishing work.

"I just... don't feel great. I need to go," Gareth says, grabbing his jacket from behind the bar and throwing it on before leaving.

"That was weird," Ollie says, finishing his pint and putting the glass back on the bar.

"No kidding," I say and pout him up another pint as the couple who just walked in join him in the queue. I finish with his drink and Ollie takes a seat at one of the high tables by the bar and leaves me to clear the customers. One orders a flight of all the ales we have on offer, and the other orders a glass of wine. Easy selections, so I finish them quickly and clear the queue. Everyone takes their seats and gets settled away, so I can join Ollie at his table.

"Do you think... he's been acting a bit weird?" I ask.

"You know Gareth better than I do," Ollie says. "But

honestly yeah, I think he's been acting a bit funny. Especially today when you mentioned Carl. He was fine before you mentioned him."

I sit and think about what he's saying for a moment. I wonder if he's coming to the same conclusion I am.

"When did Gareth finish work on Wednesday night?" he asks.

"I think he closed up at midnight. The game ran a little later than usual, because Carl got into a fight from someone on the other team. So they had to pause the game and have a little breather."

"And we know that Carl was killed after midnight, right?"

"Yes, he had to be. Otherwise, someone would have seen him last night."

"Why didn't you see him this morning?" Ollie asks.

"I went a different direction. Sometimes if I have to run errands in the morning or stop for a coffee, I'll take the bus or walk through town," I say.

"What time did Gareth get here?"

"He was late."

"Isn't that a little strange?" he asks.

"No. He and his wife have a small child. He's often up in the morning with his daughter, so sometimes he has to do the drop off to nursery and he'll go back to sleep until work. And he wasn't *that* late," I say.

"Hm," Ollie considers what I'm saying.

You know, maybe Gareth isn't being completed honest. Ollie is right, Gareth did storm out today. And I know Gareth always takes the footpath home. It's the quickest way home and he never wants to waste money on a taxi.

There was no way that he could have walked to work this morning without Carl's body.

So did he see it and not say anything? Or was something much worse at play?

"We can't just… accuse Gareth of murder," I say.

A small queue has formed at the bar, so I excuse myself and pour up their drinks.

"Have you heard what happened to Carl?" Susanne, one of the regular customers, asks as I pour up her white wine. She and her husband always come for a drink after they close up their work working shop next to us. She's been a customer here for decades, so I know her well.

"I did. I was the one who found him this morning, actually," I say.

"Absolutely horrible," she says. "Nothing like that ever happens around here. How did you find him? The police haven't released a lot of information yet."

I don't know what I should or shouldn't say. But the police didn't tell me to keep anything to myself, so I guess I can tell her what I know.

"He was just lying across the footpath across town. I probably would've seen him earlier except I took the bus to work. I was tired and didn't fancy the walk. Then I spilt beer and I had to go home to get changed. I wanted to walk Lady, so we took the footpath. Anyway, it didn't seem new. Like he'd been there for a few hours."

"Do you know how he died?" she asks.

"No. There was no blood or anything. He was just on his side on the footpath. I wouldn't doubt if he died from natural causes," I say, but Suzanne looks sceptical.

"I heard he had poison in his system. I didn't want to

say this, but… I heard him and Gareth talking when I was here on Wednesday night," she says.

Suzanne isn't on the darts team, but she still comes in for her evening glass of wine and to get some gossip, so I'm not surprised she overheard the conversation.

"I heard Carl telling Gareth that he better come up with the money he owed him. Or that Gareth would be in trouble."

"Gareth owed Carl money?" I ask, just to make sure I'm understanding her correctly.

"He did. Something about a bet gone wrong. Carl made it seem like Gareth owed him the money for a long time, and Carl wasn't going to allow it any longer," she says.

Suzanne takes her glass of wine and her husband's draft beer and takes them over to the table once she realises she won't get any more information from me.

I pour myself a shandy. Half a pint of German lager mixed with half a pint of lemon lime soda. It sounds strange, but it's refreshing and low in alcohol, so I don't mind having one at work. Normally I do that at the end of the day, but I think today has been particularly stressful, so I don't mind having one. I bring Ollie another beer as well and settle back down with him to discuss the situation at hand.

"I have some new information," I say before recapping everything that Suzanne told me.

"I think something has to be done about this," Ollie says when he finally digests what I've told him.

"Should we talk to him?" I ask.

"No. We need to go right to the police," he says.

I spend the rest of my shift on pins and needles. I want to go right to the police, but with Gareth gone, I have no one to watch the bar. Luckily, we close early on Thursdays, so at eight, I shut the bar and Ollie and I get across town to the police station as quickly as possible.

I've never been inside a police station before, so I expected it to be a lot busier. But for the most part, it looks like any other office. No criminals yelling that they're innocent, or guards walking around with keys clanking on their belts.

Ollie and I take a number even though we're the only ones there and sit in the waiting area.

"You can't bring that dog in here," the officer at the desk says when we enter the police station.

I look down at Lady, who looks back up at me. She's used to being around me and will panic if I leave her alone. I decide to just ignore that and continue with my information.

"I think I know who murdered Carl," I say.

"Let me get Officer Wilson," she says.

A couple of minutes later, we get ushered into an interview room. Lady quietly walks behind me, trying not to draw too much attention to herself. Ollie and I sit down at the table in the middle of the room and Lady makes herself as small as possible at our feet.

"I didn't expect to see you again so quickly about this, Gemma," Officer Wilson says. "What do you have for me?"

"We think Gareth might have killed Carl," I say.

I give Officer Wilson all the evidence we have.

"It's not much," he says. "It is interesting that he was

at Henderson's and then the next morning he was found poisoned. And there is some interesting circumstantial evidence around Gareth and Carl's relationship... but other than that, we don't have a lot. Really, we're going to need physical evidence that ties him to the case. I appreciate you coming in today, I know you were trying to help. But Gemma, Ollie... please stay out of this. I know you worked as a big city lawyer, Gem, but you were a corporate solicitor. Not a detective."

He's right. I know the law, but not criminal law. I would have loved to be a detective, but I wanted the big city life. Until I actually had it. Now I'm happier as a pub owner back in my small village.

I feel deflated. I don't know how I can work alongside Gareth if I think he's a murderer. Besides, I need to make sure I protect my customers.

But I don't know if he's actually done anything wrong. I certainly can't fire him unless I get some actual evidence that anyone is at risk. He has a family to support, after all.

"Look, Gemma, I'll look into it. I'll at least talk to Gareth and see what he says. But please be careful. Accusations like this can really ruin a man's life," he says.

I feel a pang of guilt. He's right — even though I think there is a strong possibility that it actually was Gareth.

Lady and I say goodbye to Ollie on the way out of the police station before going home. I don't want to walk on the footpath alone, but at least I have a dog with me, which helps me feel safer. And Lady could use the walk, really. With everything going on, I haven't had time to do our usual walks in the woods or games of fetch.

I forgot about the laundry yesterday, so I take it outside to hand on the clothesline to freshen it up. I look over the back garden and the wooded area surrounding the footpath. It's dark, but I can see lights in the distance.

Lights belonging to CCTV cameras.

The next morning, I stop by the pet shop on the way to work to get Lady a treat. She adores everyone at the pet shop, we go at least once a week to replace her favourite ball which she has a habit of destroying.

"Good morning," I say when we walk in the small shop. Lady immediately puts her paws up on the counter to ask the owner for a treat, which she gets.

"Back for another ball?" Rosa, the shop owner, asks.

"I'll grab one while we're here. But mostly I came in to say hi. And to give Lady her usual visit and treat," I say. Lady loves the toys at Rosa's shop, and she destroys at least one squeaky ball a month.

"It's always nice to have her. I have the best job in Dover, you know. I try to deal with the pets as much as possible — the less human interaction I have, the better," she laughs.

"I can imagine," I say.

"Did you hear what happened to Carl? And so close by, too."

"That's what I'm here for, actually. I have a favour to ask you."

"Of course, anything."

"Do you have the CCTV footage for that night? I just wanted to see if there was anything of interest on it."

"Do you think my CCTV might have picked something up? It would never be able to see the footpath," Rosa says.

"No, but maybe someone was coming by this way. I think I know about what time it would have happened."

"Should I call the police?" she asks.

I don't want them to know I'm still poking around about this case and get in trouble. Besides, Rosa might not have anything.

"No, I'm… helping Officer Wilson out. He has a lot on his plate, and he knows I used to be a solicitor in the city. So I'm just helping for now."

Welp. I'm in deep now with that lie.

"Of course. I'll pull it up. Can I email it over to you? I have some click and collect orders I need to get done, but as soon as those are done, I'll send them right over to you. I want to help as much as I can."

I give Rosa my email address, and Lady and I continue to work.

For once, Gareth has arrived at Henderson's before I have and he has opened up shop.

"Morning," I say cautiously. I have no idea what kind of a mood he will be in.

"Morning," he says.

"How have you been?"

"Well… I had a bit of a rough morning," he says, "I was called into the police station."

"Oh?" I try to act surprised.

"What did you tell them, Gemma?" he lets out in a huff.

"Nothing, I—"

" —I've known you for over a decade," he says, "I can tell when you're lying. Officer Wilson said that there were some issues with me at work, and someone thought I was involved in Carl's death. You would be the only one who knows about any issues at work. So please be honest with me, what did you tell them?"

"I was just... sorry, Ollie found out that you owed Carl some money. Something about a bet gone wrong. And we know that you've been late to work. I just... jumped to conclusions, I think."

"It's fine," Gareth says, "I didn't do it. I promise. Yes, I was in some financial trouble. But I came clean about it to my wife, and we're getting through it. I wouldn't kill any-one because of some money being owed. I have a young daughter; I can't do that to her. Besides, I was at home all night with my wife. We have security cameras outside the home, showing I got in after work and didn't leave until the morning. I took a taxi home, so I was home just a cou-ple of minutes after locking up the pub. I have the receipt for the taxi, the police know it wasn't me."

He's completely right. And he knows I would help him if needed. Henderson's doesn't make a lot of money, but if he needed more hours or even a pay rise or an advance on his pay, I would make sure it happened. And he's a smart guy, he can get himself out of a lot of situations. And I'm just so glad that it wasn't him.

"I just really want to find out who did it. I can't sleep knowing there's a killer on the loose," I say.

"We'll find him," he says.

"Officer Wilson does not want me to go looking. But...

well, I might have another lead already," I say.

"Cheers to that," he says and tips his water bottle at me before taking a swig. "Tell me all about it."

I'm on pins and needles all day, periodically checking my phone for an email from Rosa.

A couple of hours into shift, the email finally comes through:

Hi, Gemma. I've attached the CCTV footage for the camera facing the footpath on the night that Carl died. I've watched it and I don't see much, but maybe you can do more with this than I can.

- Rosa

I open the attached document and start scrubbing through the footage. I can see Carl, wearing what he wore every week to darts — a pair of blue jeans and his navy-blue waxed jacket.

A couple of minutes later, someone else appears on the screen. Someone wearing a long black jacket and a paperboy cap. I can't see the person's face, but the build looks like a man.

"Do you know who this is?" I ask Gareth and show him the video on my phone.

"He looks familiar... I wish we had better lighting," he says, taking the phone and holding it closer to his face to get a better look. "I really don't know who that is. Sorry." He hands the phone back to me.

I can't believe we have a video of someone following Carl onto the footpath the night he died, but we have no idea who he is. It feels like I've never been closer but also never been further from having answers.

The doorbell chimes and I see Ollie walk through the

front door.

"Any big updates?" he asks.

"I think so. We have a video of Carl the night he died, and it looked like there was someone following him, but we don't know who it is," I say.

"Let me take a look," Ollie says, and I show him the video.

"That person looks so familiar. I'm sure I've seen someone just like that…"

He rewinds and watches the video again, staring intently at the screen.

"You know… It looks like someone I might know. Well, yeah, there might be someone else it could be. And that person looks a lot like this. The hat looks so familiar," Ollie says, taking a long drink of his ale.

Gareth and I exchange a look.

"…who?" I ask carefully.

"Well, he's not a dangerous guy. Him and Carl just weren't really friends," Ollie says.

"Who?" I ask again.

"James. He doesn't come around here a lot. He owns the auto repair shop in town, so not far from here at all."

"What did James have against him?" Gareth asks.

"He played for one of the rival darts teams. Henderson's beat the Black Dog last week. Carl threw the winning dart, actually. There was a little bit of an argument, James said he was over the line when he threw," Ollie says.

"Would he really kill someone over that?" I ask.

"You never know," Gareth says. "People get angry about a lot of things. I know I had to escort James out more than once on darts nights," he says.

Wow, I had no idea they got so rowdy. I need to keep a better eye on the CCTV cameras we have in here. I never work on Wednesday nights, but apparently I need to come in and keep an eye on the darts players.

"Maybe we should go talk to him," I say. "Gareth, can you watch the bar please?"

He looks around, cleaning one of the glasses from the dishwasher. There are no customers here except Ollie.

"I think I can manage, boss," he says.

I ignore the subtle dig and go get my coat and Lady's lead. When she sees it, she jumps up, ready to go home for the day.

"We're going on a little adventure," I tell her as I clip the leash on.

Ollie and I set off down the old high street. Henderson's is situated on the corner of the pedestrian only street at the top of a large hill. The street was the major shopping centre for the town, long before cars had any place here, which is why the street is so windy and narrow.

Ollie and I walk past the small souvenir shops and cafés that line the old high street and turn right at the end of the road. This part of the town, near the harbour, is much more modernized. We keep walking until we find James' garage.

I've only been here once before, and that was to get the oil changed in my dad's old car. It needed some work that he kept putting off, and when I got all his old things, I kept the car. I hate driving, I'd been living in London for too long. But now I need to transport items for the pub, so I had to get used to using it.

We approach the garage. I have no idea where to find

James. I know he owns the place, so will he be in a manager's office? Or working on one of the cars? I doubt I'll be allowed to walk around in here freely. I walk up to the front desk and speak to the woman working.

"Afternoon. Is the owner here by any chance?" I ask.

"Do you have an appointment?" she says, opening the appointment book in front of her.

"On, no," I say, "I was just wondering if… we could talk."

"What do you need to talk about? Actually, it doesn't matter. If you want to see him, you're going to need an appointment," she says, closing the book.

Ollie and I exchange a look. I hope he's getting what I'm trying to give — we can't tip him off that we're snooping around, but we need to do our own investigating.

I drop Lady's lead and she shoots off into the garage.

"Get that dog out of here!" the receptionist shouts.

"Sorry, I'm so sorry," I say, running into the auto shop after Lady.

She runs into one of the offices — James isn't there, but his hat and jacket are hung up on the coat rack. The exact same coat and hat that the man in the video were wearing. Lady sits down next to them, panting and wagging her little brown tail.

"Good girl," I whisper and scratch behind her ear.

I take a picture of the coat rack and pick Lady's lead up and walk her out of the auto shop.

"Sorry," I say sweetly and get out of there before we draw any more attention to ourselves.

"You're never going to believe what we saw in there," I tell Ollie and fill him in on everything as we walk back up the hill to Henderson's.

"We need to go to the police," Ollie says. "I think we have enough evidence now. We have video of him, he's the only other person that was on the footpath when Carl was. He has a motive. We don't know exactly how it happened, but that's what the police are for, they'll interrogate him."

"Lady, do you want to go back to the police station?" I ask and her ears perk up.

Ollie and I march into the police station. When the officer at the desk calls our number, we're ushered into a private room and the door closed behind us. Officer Wilson lets himself in the room a couple of minutes later

"So, I understand you have some information on Carl's death. I'll be honest, this visit is coming at a bit of a surprise," he says. "I thought you were done this investigation."

"I was asking around, and well…" I say, trailing off, not sure how to tell him that I think a member of our community killed an innocent man.

"We think it was James. The owner of Easy Fix," Ollie says. I realise now I don't know James' last name. To me, he was always 'James who owned the garage'.

"James is a good man. He's lived in Dover his whole life, you know. What makes you think that it was him?" Officer Wilson asks.

"He and James had a falling out at darts on Wednesday. They were drunk and angry," I say.

"I know James, and I don't think he would kill anyone over a game of darts," Officer Wilson says. "Do you have any other reason why he would do something like this?"

"No, I think he just got mad, but…"

"I need some evidence before I accuse someone," he says.

"He was at Henderson's that night. We don't know what time Carl died, but it had to be after midnight, right? Plenty of people use that footpath to get across town after the pubs close. We have CCTV of him walking behind Carl toward the footpath the night of the murder," I say.

This finally gets Officer Wilson's attention.

"Can I see the video please? And any other evidence that you think might be relevant."

James' court date is set for just a couple of weeks later. There isn't much on the docket at the moment, and a murder trial will take the top of the list. I think the local courts just want to get it done so the newspapers will stop running stories about it. We depend a lot on tourism in the summer, so everyone wants this case to be settled before the summer rush.

Ollie and I decide to attend the sentencing. Part of me need the confirmation that it's actually James behind bars, and that we're safe again. By the looks of it, most of the town have come out as well.

The judge gets back with his sentence very quickly. With the CCTV footage from the pet shop, there's pretty solid evidence against him. James' interrogation was also pretty damning — he admitted to fighting with Carl the night of the murder, and that he slipped something into his drink. He swore that he didn't want Carl to die, but it was an accident. I don't think the jury bought it, because innocent men don't carry fatal drugs on them in case of a bar fight. I think he meant to kill him, and followed him to the footpath to make sure the job was done.

We hear the sentence and start filing out of the courtroom. James gets twenty years, eligible for parole after ten years.

"Well, Gemma. I guess I owe you an apology," Officer Wilson says as we step outside.

"It's fine," I say. "I think I also owe an apology for sticking my nose in an active murder investigation. It's just that those types of things don't often happen here, and I just couldn't help myself, I guess."

"Well, you're not a bad amateur detective. So thank you for the help. But I hope it never happens again," he says and gives me a small wave before leaving.

Lady and I spend the afternoon in a local café having a coffee and reading before getting ready for work.

Gareth arrives for work right on time and turns the sign back over to open. With everything that's gone on in the past couple of weeks, I breathe a sigh of relief. It's finally just me, my friend, Lady, and our ales.

"We have a new blonde ale," I say and take out two half pint glasses.

"Which one is this?" he asks.

"It's the new Mad Cat. It's called Blonde Ambition," I say.

"I can't believe the boss is drinking at work," he laughs. He knows that I have a beer or two at the end of each shift, but almost never at the beginning of shift.

"Listen, after the past month, I think we deserve it," I say and pour us each a drink. We sit down next to the roaring fireplace. It'll take a couple of hours before regulars start flooding in after work, but I like to have us here in the daytime in case any tourists wander up from the beach. And it gives me plenty of time to complete admin work.

"I'm really sorry about before," I say. "I just really thought that…"

"It's fine," Gareth says, "I know it looked bad. And I told my wife about everything. We're getting out of the debt and I'm making sure that it doesn't happen again. Being accused of murder was a bit of a wake-up call," he says. My face flushes with embarrassment. I know what he's like, and I know he wouldn't hurt anyone, but I think I got caught up in the excitement and wanted to be the one to save the day. At least now we can relax, the right person is behind bars.

"To finally having a peaceful day," Gareth says and raises his glass slightly before taking a sip.

"To no more death in Dover," I say and take a long drink.

Lady raises her head slightly and looks at me before lying out by the fire and closing her eyes.

Mark Squibb

For the last ten years, Mark Squibb has worked as a print and radio journalist. He is from Carbonear, Newfoundland.

'Murder at The Coffee Shop" is his first piece of prose fiction.

Murder at The Coffee Shop

"I think I'll try that cappuccino today," mused Cormac Squires, pulling his overcoat over his broad shoulders.

Each morning, the retired postal worker walked the short distance to Cedarwood Café, the small café down the street and around the corner, where he ordered a black coffee and scoured the local newspaper. The ritual complete, he would trudge back home, only to return the next day for his black coffee and newspaper.

But today, he decided, he would mix things up. The owners had recently put up money for a fancy new espresso machine, proffering lattes and cappuccinos and macchiatos and other foreign sounding beverages.

Beverley Wall, co-owner of the business, who spent as much time at the cash register as she did in the office, had been playfully pressuring him to try one of the new drinks. Residents of Biscay Bay were, it seemed, were not inclined to frothy beverages, and had to be nudged along.

"Maybe tomorrow, Bev, maybe tomorrow," he would say. "But for today, just the regular."

It appeared then, that tomorrow had finally come.

Cormac, now carefully locking the front door behind

him, did not have any social media profiles. He didn't see the need for a Facebook profile or a Twitter account (Sorry, an 'X' account). Had he either of these accounts he would have seen the circulating photos of his beloved neighbourhood café, cordoned off with police tape, flashing police lights reflecting in the storefront windows.

Had he seen the photos, he would have gone all the same, and in double time.

"More tea?" asked Cormac.

The man to whom he addressed this was Hector Pryne, the detective assigned to the case and, coincidentally, a long-standing member of the same Kin Club to which Cormac belonged.

"No, I'm good, Cormac," replied Pryne, his face drawn tight in consternation.

The two men sat in silence a moment longer before Pryne relented.

"Alright, Cormac, I'll tell you what I know," said Pryne. "But only because I know you don't mean any harm and because you knew the girl. Also... it seems you have a knack for these things. But this doesn't leave here, okay?"

"Yes, yes of course," said Cormac impatiently. "Get on with it then."

"The deliveryman was the first on the scene," said Pryne. "He typically delivers to the store on Thursday, but he was a day early this week due to a scheduling conflict. He said he hadn't thought to call ahead to let anyone know as it's a smaller delivery. When he arrived, he went through the backdoor as usual. The security alarm was ringing. He found Jeff, that's the co-owner, bent over Beverley. Delivery driver says he knew that she was dead the moment he saw her. She had been stabbed twice. Lots of knives in the building, but none matching the victim's wounds. They all tested clean for blood as well, so we've no murder weapon. Nothing appeared to have been stolen from the store. And that's about all we know."

"You interviewed Jeff of course?"

"Yes, he said he arrived and found her murdered," said Pryne. "He says the delivery driver showed up just a few moments later."

"Any suspects?"

"Well, Jeff told the police that they've recently had to let go of a young woman, Silvia Madden," said Pryne. "Some $250 in cash had gone missing from the register. Jeff says that he and Bev both believed that this young woman might have pocketed it herself. We've spoken with her of course, and she of course denies both."

Cormac, being a regular at Cedarwood Café, of course knew Silvia. He remembered her as a chatty and gossipy, but not unkind, voluble but not offensive.

"Alibi?" asked Cormac.

"She clocked in for her shift — and no I will not tell you where she works lest you badger her— at 7 a.m. Plenty of witnesses," said Pryne. "However, there's no accounting for her whereabouts prior to that. She says she drove straight to work. But there's no roommate or boyfriend to collaborate the story. It seems unlikely that she could have committed the murder, drove home again, changed, and then drove to work, all before 7 a.m. but, even accounting for driving time, not impossible."

"And the money?"

"Still missing."

"Any other suspects?"

"There's a man from one of the shelters that hangs around the store most mornings—"

"Yes, Johnny. He seems harmless. Usually bums a few bucks and then goes on his way."

"Yeah, that's him. He says he didn't show up that morning until after the police had arrived. Says he never saw anything."

"Yes, I spoke with Johnny myself that morning," said Cormac. "He arrived just after I did. He seemed genuinely shocked, and I don't believe he was putting on an act — although one really doesn't know I suppose."

Cormac considered all this for a moment.

"Any thing else?" he asked.

"Stephanie Walsh, a friend of the victim, showed up later that morning. She said she drove in to town that morning and that that victim had been expecting her. Text messages between the two seem to bear that out. Again, nothing concrete to tie her to the scene."

Cormac sat still a moment, head in his hands, digesting all the information, before addressing the detective once again.

"There's one other thing that's bothering me," said Cormac

"And what's that?" asked Pryne.

"The alarm system," said Cormac

Cormac would say no more, leaving Pryne to his own stipulations.

"Cormac! How lovely to see you again!"

Cormac smiled up at the young woman in the mint green waitress outfit and hair bun.

"Silvia, it's good to see you again too. I didn't know you worked here."

'Here' was Templeton's Bar and Grill, and Cormac had in fact known that Siliva worked there — a couple of casual phone calls to some friends around town nailed that down pretty quickly.

In fact, Cormac was at the restaurant this day just to see her.

"Yes, sweetie, since September, not long after I left Cedarwood."

Cormac noted that in Silvia's telling of the tale she was not fired from the cafe, but left of her own accord.

"Oh, isn't it terrible what happened?" said Silvia, her face darkening. "Poor Bev. I mean, I had my disagreements with Bev and Jeff both — they never came outright and said it, but they seemed to think I stole from the registers, if you can believe that! — but they both were okay, really."

He smiled. Silvia, he though, had always been an open book.

"Of course, the police interviewed me — although I guess it was more of an interrogation, wasn't it? — I mean of course they knew that I had only left recently, so I was a natural suspect," said Silvia. "It was terrible!"

The gleam of excitement in her eye told Cormac that she was more thrilled than horrified to be considered a suspect in a murder investigation.

"I suppose they asked your all sorts of things?" asked Cormac.

"Oh, just if I had spoken with the victim — Bev— recently — which I hadn't — and where I was that morning, which was here of course" said Silvia.

Cormac smiled, and then placed his order.

Cormac rang the doorbell in front of him and then quickly thrust his hand back into the deep pockets of his overcoat, his breath billowing like plumes of smoke in the cold weather.

He was about to ring again when he heard a shuffling sound from inside, and a moment later Jeff Strong was standing before him

"Cormac, come inside," said Jeff, opening the door for the man twice his size and twice his age and ushering him into the narrow front porch.

"I hate to be a bother," began Cormac. "Just with everything with Bev, I just wanted to stop by. How are you doing?"

"I mean, it's a shock," said Jeff. "I just don't know. It doesn't seem real. Here, come upstairs and have a seat."

Jeff led the Cormac up the steps and into an open concept kitchen and dining room, where a young blonde woman sat at the dining table, a mug of steaming coffee before her.

"Cormac, this is Stephanie," said Jeff with a gesture of his hand. "Stephanie, this is Cormac. He is — or was — one of our regulars."

"Pleased to meet you," said Cormac, extended his hand to the young woman. Cormac noted the firm, businesslike handshake.

"I'm sorry, if I had known you had company I wouldn't have stopped by," said Cormac, blushing faintly.

"No, no it's fine," returned Stephanie. "I drove into town the morning... well, you know, the morning of. I just couldn't believe it... Bev and I had texted that night before and I had plans to stay for a few days... I just didn't know what to do so I'm staying here with Jeff for a few days, at least until the police have figured something out. It's cheaper than staying at a hotel at least."

"We have some coffee cake, Cormac, would that do?" asked Jeff, bustling around the kitchen.

"Make sure to use the cake knife if you're slicing the cake Jeff, not the streak knife," Stephanie called from the table. "And please wipe the crumbs off before dropping the knife in the sink."

A few minutes later — coffee poured, cake sliced, and knife wiped free of crumbs before being dropped into sink — all three sat around the table, trying their hand at small talk before Cormac finally broached the subject of Bev's murder.

"We all know who did it," said Jeff, his face flushed with anger. "Madden. And the sooner the cops catch on the better."

"But what about that fellow you said hung around?" asked Stephanie. "Jack?"

"Oh Johnny? Johnny was a pain but he's harmless," said Strong. "This was Silvia's work, but at the rate the police are moving, she's going to walk free. Something ought to be done about."

Later that night, after some deliberation, Cormac dialed Jeff, who answered on the third ring.

"Hello?"

"Jeff? This is Cormac, could I meet you at the store tomorrow?"

"Cormac? What do you mean meet me at the store?"

"It's important," said Cormac. "I think I know how we can make Silvia talk."

Jeff stood, silent and dumbstruck.

"Jeff, are you there?"

"Yes, no, I'm here. Can't you tell me over the phone?"

"No, I would really rather meet you in person. Please Jeff."

"Yeah, okay, tomorrow morning. How is 7 a.m.?"

Cormac agreed to the time and hung up.

Jeff turned to Stephanie, who was staring with a quizzical look on her face.

"Well?" she asked.

"Cormac asked me to meet him at the store tomorrow. He said he knows how to make Silvia talk."

At 7 a.m. the next morning, Cormac knocked on the back door of the Cederwood Café. It was the same door the delivery driver would have entered the morning of Bev's murder just a few days before.

From inside, Cormac heard a bolt being drawn, and a moment later, Jeff opened the door and admitted him.

At the far end of the room stood Stephanie.

"Good morning, good morning," said Cormac, laying his cell phone and keys on a nearby prep table. If he felt any surprise at seeing Stephanie, he hid it well.

"Well, we're here, what's this about getting Silvia to talk?" asked Jeff.

Cormac stood still a moment, his eyes never leaving Jeff's face.

"Why did you do it, Jeff?" he finally asked, his voice weary and strained. "I guess it must have been so you could sell this place, huh?"

Jeff stood a moment in shocked silence, before uttering a dry laugh.

"You think I did this? What is this, some attempt at an ambush? You're going to try and work me over is that it?"

"I've always suspected you," said Cormac. "The delivery driver caught you red-handed as they say. You were always the most likely suspect in my mind. But what I couldn't figure out — why the alarm?"

"The alarm?" asked Jeff. "What are you getting on with?"

"The delivery driver said the alarm had been triggered. Obviously, you would have known the security code, so you wouldn't have set it off — unless, you had of course schemed to invent some tall tale about an intruder, some masked man who broke in and murdered poor Bev and set off the alarm in the process. But no. You claimed you had seen no one else in the building. Certainly, no masked intruder on whom to blame the crime. So why the alarm? It served no purpose; it seemed purely accidental.

It was not, anyway, part of the plan."

Here Cormac paused a moment before continuing.

"But then I realized you had an accomplice," said Cormac, his gaze now falling on Stephanie. "If this woman does not trust you to properly cut coffee cake or put a knife in the sink, she would not trust you to commit murder. She was here that morning, to oversee, to make sure everything was done by the book and that no mistakes were made."

Stephanie's face betrayed no emotion, and Cormac continued.

"But then, the delivery driver shows up. A day ahead of schedule," Cormac continues. "You panic. I believe you had always intended to call the police and claim to have found the body to avert suspicion from yourself. But you don't want to be discovered now, not like this. And Stephanie has no reason to be there, her presence will raise questions that will need to be answered. And so, you tell her to run, to take the knife, the murder weapon, and run out the front door. She does so, setting off the alarm in the process."

Jeff stared at Cormac with something approaching shock. Stephanie, however, had by now drawn her face into a tight, angry scowl.

"You made sure to tell the police all about Silvia and cast suspicion on her. That $250 was never recovered. However, I have an idea that if the police were to check with the Lamplighter Inn just outside of town, they would learn that a young woman arrived the night before the murder and paid cash for a single room. $250 would cover it, would it not? Because of course, Stephanie, you had to be here, didn't you? But you couldn't stay at Jeff's home, no, that would look too suspicious. People must not know you are intimately acquainted. And so, when Jeff stole that money from his own safe, he not only cast suspicion on poor Silvia, but gave you a means to arrive in town undetected. You simply had to show up the next morning and pretend you had driven in that morning."

Cormac sighed deeply.

"I believe that's everything," he said finally, just to fill the silene.

Another beat of quiet, and then a scream of rage. Stephanie, her eyes burning with cruel fire, let out yet another banshee shriek, before grabbing a knife off a nearby rack and throwing herself towards Cormac.

She had cleared half the room, knife raised high, both Cormac and Jeff too stunned to move, when Pryne burst through the back door, service pistol raised.

"Freeze! Dropped the weapon!" he cried, pistol raised high.

Stephanie stood for a moment, stunned, and then dropped the knife and began to weep.

Neither of them had noticed, when Cormac had set his cell phone down, that a call had been in progress.

"That was risky, you know?" said Pryne in a tone reserved for scolding small children.

"Yes, I know... but it had to be done, didn't it?" said Cormac, setting down his tea. "I'm just glad you agreed to wait outside on standby or else you would have had a second murder at the coffee shop to investigate. Everything check out I imagine?"

"Yes," replied the detective. "The clerk at the Lamp-lighter positively identified the Walsh girl. She paid cash for a room the night before the murder. And we found the knife at the Strong residence. Tossing it was too risky I suppose — better to hide it in plain sight. Jeff admitted that following Bev's murder, he had planned to sell the business. Seemed he had wanted out for some time but couldn't legally terminate the lease agreement without Bev's signature. And so, he killed her instead. He was led on by that Walsh girl, a regular Lady Macbeth. Following Wall's death, Strong would maintain complete ownership the business to do as he liked. I imagine he would have sold it, citing the murder."

Cormac sighed wearily. Such a waste of a life, and over such a small matter.

Ryan Belbin

Ryan Belbin is an author from Pasadena, Newfound-land, whose previous writing credits include "Cause and Effect" for *Paragon III* and "Summer Memories" for *Grenfell Inkpot*.

Previously his work appeared in *Dystopia from the Rock* with the tale "Matches" and in *Fairy Tales from the Rock* with "Bedtime Stories."

Ryan says that, before getting a job where he has to wear ties and tuck in his shirt, he spent a seven month stint hitchhiking across New Zealand.

Allowed In

Jaysus, it's going to be a long day.

That's what Wish Forsyth first thought when the woman across the table started talking much too loudly, much too animatedly, and much too early that morning. When he said as much and she half-cocked her head and responded, "But today is one of the shortest days, isn't it?", that was when he'd known beyond any doubt what a long day it would truly be.

"So you're sure it's missing? Gone? Kaput?"

"YES!" she said with the kind of gusto that nearly knocked him over from where he sat at the kitchen table, clinging to his mug of dirty-looking coffee as though it were his last lifeline, the single vestige of hope on a dreary winter's day. It sure felt like it that morning. How much had he put away last night?

Wish didn't feel guilty, mind you. It was the Christmas season after all, the time to make merry — he had only performed his civic duty with the utmost reverence. The Tibb's Eve Dance at the Legion was a sacred event in Herring Sound, after all, a time to say, "what odds?" to inhibitions or fire regulations. Wish hadn't asked for Sherri

LeDrew to come pounding on his door just after the sun made its lazy ascent over the Gough Hills on the eastern edge of the small town, its passage this particular morning dulled considerably by an early winter's storm that held the town hostage. Nonetheless, she was on a mission, and his thoughts in the matter were the least of her concern.

Still, she was his cousin, the last of his living relations in town, and besides all that blood-is-thicker-than-water drivel, he tended to enjoy her company more than he did most people's. All of these factors boded in her favour that day.

"I can't picture the brooch myself though," he admitted, idly rubbing his temples.

Sherri chuckled. "It's not like I'm going to wear it to darts or anything. I only save it for special occasions."

"Such as?"

"Well . . ." She thought for a long pause. "I guess, truth be told, I've never actually worn it. I only got it when Mom died, and that's only been two . . . no, three years this February." Wish tried to fake a sad smile — his aunt had squarely belonged in the well-populated list of people whose company he did *not* enjoy. "Besides, it's a little bit. . . unique, I suppose, is the way to put it."

"Ugly, you mean?"

"*Unique*," she repeated. Meaning yes.

"But it had been stowed in your jewelry cabinet?"

She nodded. "In an ordinary sort of drawer. The whole thing had been tore I apart, but that was what they took."

"Any idea how much it would fetch if you were to stroll into Trader's with it?"

She thought for a moment, then gave him a number.

He did his best to maintain his composure at the fact that he hadn't fathomed the extra 0 at the end of the price tag — no small feat on the best of days, let alone that day.

"Sherri, girl, you knows I loves you to bits . . . but what are you doing here? Shouldn't you be phoning this in to the constable or something?" *And let me gracefully crawl back into bed.*

"I tried!" she pleaded. "You know what it's like, over the holidays, getting anyone to come out this far. Factor in a few traffic stops on the highway, a few lovers' quarrels bolstered by booze, and I'm not expecting anyone here before January, and by then Mom's brooch is long gone and the thief with it." Sherri's fingers danced with electric bursts of anxiety across the tabletop. "I guess I mostly just *had* to talk to someone about it, y'know?"

"I get it," Wish nodded, decidedly not getting it. The best of times, he didn't think it was his dentist's business if his teeth hurt, and while his reserved nature might be a bit of an anomaly, he still thought Sherri shared traces of that trait with him. She always struck him as someone who kept her personal affairs just that: personal. Come to think of it, he couldn't recall the last conversation of any real consequence they'd had — which suited him perfectly fine, but made this early morning outpouring more than a little unusual. Maybe the stress hadn't given her much choice.

"What does Martin think of all this?"

She scoffed. "He didn't think I should be bothering you this morning, that's for sure."

Wish suddenly liked Sherri's husband a little bit more than he thought.

"He's on night shift this week at the plant, only got home this morning. First thing he asked me was what's the point in having jewelry you never wears. Second thing he asks is whether I might have misplaced it — as if my room wasn't ransacked. He can't be helped for being stunned, I suppose. But anyway, he figured I should wait until the police could show up, but I . . ."

"Had to talk about it," Wish finished for her. "Alright then. So, run me through it, what happened when the Mummers showed up?"

Wish had mixed feelings about a crowd of half-loaded good-for-nothings barging into their neighbours' homes, wearing outlandish disguises, playing their music, and making a ruckus, not to mention expecting to raid the liquor cabinet for their misdeeds. The excuse of it being a tradition never really cut it for him. The Mummers used to scare the hell out of him as a child, and some part of that fear never seemed to leave him. He put up with it just as he put up with most things: barely.

"I was in bed," Sherri said. "Had been for about half an hour, so I was getting handy to drifting right off. Anyway, there was a pounding on the front door that wouldn't stop, so I wrapped a robe around me and went down to have a peek. I had the door open a crack before the whole crew pushed it in — half a dozen of them, stuffed clothes and busting bras, sheets with eyeholes cut in 'em, plus a clickety-clackety Hobby Horse at the lead. I told them to go home out of it, that I wasn't in that kind of Christmas spirit, not that night. I loves the old ways, you knows that, but there's a time and place, and it wasn't then."

"So I guess they just went on to the next stop and left

you to your visions of sugarplums?" Wish allowed himself a crooked grin.

"Mind now! You know that only spurred them on more — into the front porch, clamoring for drinks and for a dance. I don't know where the accordion or the ugly stick came from, but they were out."

How the band of Mummers had avoided his home Wish had no idea — he tried to think on what good deeds might have earned him that kind of luck, but he came up empty handed. He still made a note to put an extra quarter in the collection plate come Sunday, just in case.

"So they were a handful, huh?"

"I didn't stop! I poured them all a drink, told them this was it, one for the road, all of that. It was chaos — and me after having cleared everything up for Christmas, it felt like a proper desecration. They was swinging me about, glutching their booze and crying out for more with their muffled voices. It felt like I'd strolled smack dab into a nightmare — but anyway, I saw someone go up the stairs. I'd swear to it — I tried to go off to see what was going on, but I got pulled back by one of those troublemakers before I got much further, and then another one made me get him another drink, and next thing I knows I forgot all about the one who went upstairs. I figured he must have gone up to the bathroom or something, and ten minutes later they had my bottle all but empty and I finally managed to shoo them away and lock everything up for the night. Turns out my night was just beginning."

"And you figures this one who left the crowd slipped your brooch in their jumper and made off before you had a chance to catch your breath, is that the way of it? When did they come back downstairs?"

"Well," Sherri said, stopping to think for a moment. "See, the problem is, I only saw a bit of movement on the stairs, out of the corner of my eye. So I'm not rightfully sure which one of the bunch it even was — or when exactly he re-joined the other hooligans." Wish felt a groan involuntarily slip through his lips as Sherri continued. "There were three of them wearing red jumpers, and I think they was all still there when buddy went. Or maybe there were only two? I was being twirled about and back and forth to the kitchen, I didn't realize I'd have to pay such close attention. I know for a fact the one wearing the sou'wester and the big ski-doo mitts was still there the whole time, though."

"You're sure?"

"No," she said, nodding. *Pat your head and rub your belly*, Wish bitterly thought as he ran his hands through his thinning hair.

"Alright, so in other words you have no idea which one it was. Do you have any idea *who* the Mummers were?"

"I'm sure it was Clyde Maxwell and his crew," she said.

"Did they ever take their masks off?"

"Well . . ." she started. "No. But they's the only ones that go jannying these days." Twenty years ago, half the cove would have been out, and the other half waiting at home for the first half, with full intentions to switch places the next night. These days though, that wasn't the way of it — the old hands lamented the change, but at least it made Wish's hangover less excruciating that morning.

"But you see the problem here, don't you?" Wish said.

"First, you've got to figure out who were the under the masks, and *then* you've got to figure out which one of the masks took a little break from the revelry to prod around your house. You been to see them yet?"

Sherri looked aghast. "At this hour of the day? Course not! It wouldn't be proper to go barging about, asking questions!"

Wish allowed himself a moment to stare at her blankly while his hands inadvertently shook the dregs of his coffee about the mug. "Get your coat on then, let's go for a walk."

Clyde probably would have welcomed the small party with even less enthusiasm than Wish had, so he decided to cut him a bit of a break (it being Christmas, after all) and stop by Sherri's house first.

Before the collapse of the fishery, Herring Sound had been a bustling community stretching along the curvature of the coastline, the epicentre of which was the wharf. Now, it was closer to an assemblage of disparate homes that only faintly resembled a town, an isolated little place facing wilderness on one side, the ocean on the other. Every successive government assured the residents, with less and less conviction, that the town would never fall prey to resettlement. Most of the younger folks had long since left, and those who remained either worked at the hospital in Carbonear or the fish plant in Blanche Point — in other words, Herring Sound had little *raison d'etre*, but the b'ys disdained French and wouldn't have given much of a care even if they had a translation. They continued to hang onto that community with a stubbornness that either bordered on admirable or foolhardy, depending on who you asked.

The quieted tableau was even more hushed this morning after the blast of snow that had assaulted the town the previous evening. The wind continued to billow gusts in front of them, and Wish found his eyes averted more often than not as the two figures navigated the zigzag of lanes to get to Sherri's house, the only two people foolish enough to be out and about on such a morning.

They stamped their boots on the mat and Wish welcomed the tingle as warmth returned to his reddened fingers. Sherri wasted no time with offering him a hot drink or a chance to stick his hands over the woodstove — instead, she led him up the first-floor landing to a familiar hallway, bathroom at one end, linen closet alongside, and a pair of bedrooms across from one another. Wish glanced into the spare bedroom as they passed.

"You're not expecting Nance home for the holidays, are you?" The bed was made up, despite the fact that Sherri's only child had lived in Calgary for years. Most of the time when Wish came by, the spare bedroom was a pile of assorted odds and ends that didn't have a rightful place anywhere else in the house.

"Hmm? Oh, no . . . you never know who's going to stop by though!" Sherri's face had seemed to drop for a second, but she was back to her bubbly self a moment later. Wish was suddenly grateful his unexpected morning guest had only imposed herself on breakfast and not for the night as well.

As she'd said, when they entered the main bedroom

the cabinet's drawers were all flung out, the contents in disarray — a stark contrast to the meticulous order with which Sherri ran her household. Prying fingers had been in a frenzy.

"This is just how you found it then?"

She nodded vigorously. "I didn't touch a thing, except to see what was all there. I didn't want to mess with any fingerprints."

"Mm-hm. I'm sure the forensic team at the RCMP is speeding down here as we speak," Wish scoffed. Realizing it came off as unduly harsh, he added, "I doubt very much this Mummer took off his gloves."

The cabinet had half a dozen drawers, in various degrees of openness. This vantage point afforded him a slightly concealed view of rows of necklaces, earrings, and other shiny trinkets. "Nothing else was taken?" Wish asked.

"Not a thing," she said, turning to leave the room. "I checked everything."

They walked back down to the main floor. In the middle of the family room, just off the entranceway, a spruce tree brushed up against the vaulted ceiling, its boughs decked with ribbons, handmade ornaments from when Nance was a child, and glass bulbs stamped with the dates of every year from the 1980s to the present. It was a mishmash, but it was a happy one, and it commanded the full attention of the room. The furniture was pushed up alongside the walls, and with the fire going the room would have made a cozy dancefloor.

"You've already cleaned up the mess, I see," Wish said. He'd wanted to catch a tumbler at least out of place, but he had no such luck. His cousin was the only person he knew in Herring Sound without a clothesline — a polished exterior was the most anyone ever got to see. What ungodly hour had she risen at all?

Sherri laughed. "We got all that snow, so there was a mess of water in the living room to mop up, and a few glasses to stick in the dishwasher. But other than that, for all the trouble they caused, they were reasonably behaved." She stopped for a moment. "I mean, besides the obvious."

"Of course."

"Sherlock 'Olmes having any luck?" Martin LeDrew, bracing a mug of coffee with a meaty forearm against a beer belly, emerged from the kitchen into the living room. His pyjama pants and unshaven face made him appear a different species from his wife, who looked like she'd spent a chunk of the morning doing herself up before she'd rushed over to Wish's. Not for the first time that day, he wondered what time she must have risen.

"You had a bit of nasty luck with the merrymakers last night?" Wish commented.

"Seems to be the way of it. Some clown with a few too many drinks in 'im, got a little bit bold — I don't doubt that once his 'eavy 'ead subsides we'll have a repentant Mummer on 'and."

"A little bit bold? Come off it, Martin, the room was tore apart! This was deliberate *and* malicious, you knows that!" Sherri countered in a way that felt more like a continuation of an earlier disagreement than a new melee.

Her husband rolled his eyes. "Gaudy sort of piece, woulda stuck out like a sore thumb on every stitch of clothing you own. Can't imagine what worth buddy woulda seen in it."

"That's not the point a'tall!" Sherri exclaimed.

"Imagine keeping something like that, not even locked away. Sure you should have listened to me ages ago and insured the thing."

"My God, Martin, what state is the world coming to that I need to keep everything I own under lock and key from folks I've known since I was a child? I never would have believed the day that this kind of thing could happen in my own home!"

"That's all well and good, but you *never* stop to think about what might 'appen, and it would be so easy to just make a little effort and—"

Wish stepped in, lest things escalate any further — he doubted whether his head could handle it. "Right. Least we can do is go have a chat with young Maxwell. We're up and about, it's not hurting anything. What do you say?"

"You go ahead," Martin said, having a hefty gulp of his coffee. "I've got enough things around here to keep me busy without playing detective all day."

"S'pose waiting for your supper to be cooked and staying out of your own way is a full-time job," Sherri muttered as she slipped her coat back on and bent over to lace up her boots.

Safely stored in a heated garage throughout the winter, the '85 Eldorado was a beauty; two lawyers as parents was not without its perks, especially when it came to fancy toys. The first thing Wish thought, when Clyde

Maxwell pushed himself out from beneath the polished blue front of the car on an old wooden creeper, was that young people had it much too easy. He still felt like hell after half a bottle of rum the night before, but the only sign that anything was off on the younger man was a faint red tinge to his eyeballs. He seemed in good enough spirits.

"Whaddy'at b'ys?" He grinned. "Sherri LeDrew, out for another dance 'er what? You'll have to give me a few minutes, get cleaned up a bit."

"Grow up, Clyde," she groaned, arms crossed tight about her chest.

"Where's the fun in that?" he said, still lying flat on his back looking up at them upside-down. There was redness in his eyes, no question about it, but the dominant feature was that of mischief, a glint that was unmistakable.

Wish bent down so that he was hovering just above Clyde. He hung onto the hood of the Cadillac to give him something to steady himself — he hoped (perhaps somewhat in vain) that he looked more menacing than he felt. "You make off with more than just a buzz last night?"

Wish had planned to play it cooler than that, but the sudden sight of Clyde Maxwell, the smug look on his face, coupled with his own massive hangover on a blustery Christmas Eve when he should have been in bed, just managed to set him over the edge. At least it took the smirk off Clyde's face for a second, so there was that.

"What are you talkin' about?" he asked. To his credit, it seemed genuine.

"A member of your little troupe went rooting through some drawers last night," Wish said, ignoring the sudden return of Clyde's smirk, "so we wanted to know if you knew anything about it."

Clyde pushed himself the rest of the way out from under the car and ambled to his feet. He did so, Wish noticed, much more gracefully than he had lowered himself onto his haunches. When he did, he came about a head higher than Wish. "Are you 'sinuating anything? You callin' me a thief?"

Now it was Sherri who had to step in to quell an early morning fire. "That's not what we're about a'tall! Besides," she said, turning to Wish, "Clyde was the one with the Hobby Horse, he is every year. He never left the living room."

It might have been nice to have mentioned that before now. God, his head hurt.

"Be that as it may," Wish said, fighting to regain some composure, "one of your friends robbed Sherri last night."

"That doesn't sound like any of my friends," Clyde replied matter-of-factly.

"Who was with you last night?" Sherri asked.

He switched back again to the grinning kid looking to start some trouble. "Those aren't the rules, you knows that. You're supposed to guess."

"Jaysus," Wish said, not caring if Clyde Maxwell was five feet taller than him and had three hundred pounds on him. "Come off it b'y, you think we wants to be at this, today of all days? Can't you just help us out so we can get out of here and leave you be?"

Clyde chewed over it for a minute. He carried more than his share of youthful arrogance, and he didn't think anyone, let alone a couple of folks old enough to be his parents, had any right to come onto his turf and accuse him of things he hadn't done. On the other hand, he liked the idea of being rid of them and getting back to his solitude.

"It was me, Carol Hann, Skip and Sid Arbuckle, Bruce Pynn, Lisa Tobin, and Buckey Brake. Like I said, though, none of them are the sorts to be getting into late-night heists." He bent back down again, clearly of the opinion that he had given his input and that the discussion was over. As if to confirm, he wheeled back beneath the vehicle, and the next sound was that of a ratchet twisting.

"Let's be on our way then," said Wish, turning to leave.

The ratchet suddenly stopped, and Clyde wheeled himself back out from under the vehicle. "Oh, Sherri, say hello to Nance for me, wouldja?" He gave her a wink that spurred her out the door quicker than if he'd gotten up and given her a push.

They stood on the Tobin's doorstep, a monolithic saltbox right alongside the water, blowing on their hands and kicking their feet. The morning had nearly passed, and the squalls were getting increasingly agitated, joined by the icy prickle of salt spray.

The Arbuckle twins were still in bed when Wish and Sherri showed up, and their old man was not about to go waking them up. Bruce Pynn had dated Nance for close to two years in high school, and they ended things on good terms — Sherri had no intention of coming anywhere handy to accusing him of anything, unless there was no other choice. Carol Hann and Buckey Brake lived in St.

John's and still went together, but were back in Herring Sound for the holiday and staying with Carol's parents farther along the shore.

So, they waited for someone, anyone, to open the door and let them in out of the cold.

From behind the peeling paint of the heavy door, a face concealed in shadows peaked out, trepidation as palpable as the odour of fish gurry on a hot summer afternoon. The door almost shut again, but Wish swung out his hand and braced it. "Merry Christmas, Madge."

Madge Tobin, looking older than her 50-odd years, resigned and pulled back the door. "Christmas, Wish. Sherri. Whaddya want?"

On any other day, Madge's briskness would have been endearing to Wish. He had never forgotten that, for one very fleeting summer, before he dropped out of school, they had very nearly become a serious item and could well have made a go of it. Their worldviews certainly aligned in more than a few ways — alas, it had never been, and didn't seem to trouble anyone one little bit, but he couldn't help but think of it as he stood outside her porch.

"Is Lisa home?" Sherri asked, shifting her body to invite herself in.

"She's just finishing breakfast. What's you want to see 'er for?"

"She out late last night?" Sherri continued, ignoring the question or the gradual suspicious squinting on Madge's face.

Wish, feeling a mixture of commiseration for Madge (knowing full well what it was like to be woken by Sherri's insistence) and certainty the door was about to get slammed in his face, spoke up. "There was a bit of an incident last night, at Sherri's house. I think Lisa was out with the gang, doing some jannying?"

"What kind of h'incident?" That had piqued her curiosity, and maybe a bit of worry.

"Can we speak to her?" Sherri insisted, stepping forward now and wedging her feet between the open door and the frame, firmly across the threshold. "Please, Madge. It's important."

That had done it. She nodded, opened the door wider. "She's in the kitchen."

Wish and Sherri brushed the snow from their coats and moved into the home, which was scarcely warmer than the outside air. Lisa Tobin was slumped at the kitchen table, bent over a half-eaten piece of toast, holding her face in her hands and silently shaking.

"Jeez girl, cheer up, would ya? There's a few folks here to see you," Madge said, moving past Wish and Sherri and scooping up the toast and tossing it into the bin beneath the sink. Wish and Sherri looked to each other, shrugging their shoulders.

"Sorry," Madge said, turning to them. "Imagine though. You spends your whole life in Newfoundland and you still get surprised when there's snow at the end of December."

"Mom!" Lisa yelled, looking up for the first time. Like Clyde, her eyes were red, but hers were ringed — whereas his had come from the drink, hers were clearly from sobbing. "Have a heart, would you? Just because this is a perpetually miserable, god-awful rock in the middle of the

Atlantic, you don't need to blame someone for having the gall to want to get away once every two decades or so, do you?" She burst into a fresh onslaught of tears then.

Madge shook her head. "Poor thing had it all worked out. Her and her b'yfriend were going away to one of them all-inclusives in Bermuda or Mexico or some spot for the holidays. Except, well," she cocked her head to the window. As if on cue, a fresh gust rattled the window frame. "No planes leaving town, and crews still haven't managed to open up the highways since last night. She was planning a holiday on the beach — now it looks like she'll spend one here at home, watching the *Grinch* on tape with me."

Wish resisted the urge to say that didn't sound altogether bad. Sherri, however, wasn't fazed. "So you figured you'd be thousands of kilometres away today, is that right?"

Madge's eyes narrowed. "What did you say this was all about again?"

"How many Mummers were with you last night?" Wish interrupted. Lisa looked at him intently with her red-rimmed eyes as if she were just realizing there were other people about.

"Half a dozen or so," she said. "Once things died down at the dance, the b'ys were still right on the go, so off we went."

"What were you wearing?"

Madge turned a different shade of annoyed. "It's hung out by the back porch. Over the stove."

Wish didn't wait for an invitation — grateful for an excuse to slip out of the kitchen, he rounded the corner and saw the brilliant red jumper, the DD bra, and cheesecloth with eye holes cut in it hung along pegs in the wall. The heat from the bellowing stove struck him as soon as he entered — stepping over the slumped-over galoshes on the floor, wincing as he stuck his sock right into a puddle of melted snow, he ran his hand along the damp fabric, idly shaking it as he moved along the limp silhouette of last evening's Mummer.

No visions of sugarplums danced in Wish's head, but his hangover tore away from his fuzzy brain in a flash as something clicked into place.

"Bet you could have used a nice little bonus to buy a few mojitos down south, couldn't you?" he heard from the kitchen.

"Sherri!" Wish yelled. He ran back into the kitchen and grabbed her arm, perhaps a little bit harder than he meant to.

"Madge, Lisa — sorry about that. Merry Christmas. Sherri, we should go."

"What was that all about?" Sherri demanded as they drew their coats tighter about them. The morning light had already given way to the dim afternoon slant of the sun heralding the latter part of the day. It held a melancholy feeling to it which, against the vastness of the temperamental ocean, couldn't help but give one pause. Unless they were near off their head with anxiety, in which case the sublime didn't mean a whole lot.

"I saw her Mummer costume. Want to know what it was like?"

"Half a dozen pockets and pouches to stow a brooch in, probably!"

"Wet," Wish answered. "Out in the storm last night, it must have been satched then, judging by the way it feels now."

"What's your point, Wish?" Sherri demanded.

"Come back to my house, we aren't going to argue in the weather like this. I needs to get myself a nice hot coffee too, my head is about ready to burst." That suddenly reminded him of something else — something that had hung over him all day.

"Why weren't you at the Tibb's Eve Dance last night?" he asked. It hadn't struck him as odd before now, until he realized that Sherri and Martin LeDrew *never* missed the Tibb's Eve Dance. No one in Herring Cove did as a general rule.

"What? I told you, I wasn't in the Christmas mood."

"Like I said, I needs to get myself a nice hot coffee, but as soon as I do, you're going to tell me why you've been lying to me."

After a day which, as he had predicted early on, had been quite long, it gave Wish at least a little hint of satisfaction to watch Sherri squirm in her boots as he led her back to the house, unanswered questions hanging in the air with the falling snowflakes. It was even nicer when he set the coffee maker on and asked her for Clyde Maxwell's phone number and excused himself to make a quick phone call. By the time he came back, the coffee was ready, and he settled himself in across from her at the kitchen table where the whole Christmas Eve fiasco began.

"Alright," Sherri said, as it seemed to be her turn to start, "you have my attention, and my confusion. What are you talking about, lying to you? You're not saying I had anything to do with this?"

Wish smiled into his mug and shook his head. "Nope. Nope, nope, nope. And I don't say that only because you're my cousin and I know you don't have a bad bone in your body — you had nothing to gain by pretending to steal an uninsured piece of jewelry. No, you lied, but not to deliberately shag things up. I've been working backwards since it occurred to me, and I think I understand why you did what you did — mostly because it seemed inconsequential at the time. It might not have even saved us that much headache, now I thinks of it, but still it would have been nice for you to have trusted me off the hop."

Sherri rattled her fingertips on the edge of the table, waiting for him to continue.

"Why didn't you tell me things was so bad with you and Martin?"

That clearly wasn't what she had been expecting. She stopped her rattling and her mouth hung uselessly open. "How —"

"The weather, and the spare bedroom. When we were by your place this morning, Martin was just out of bed, not just off the night shift. That might have just been a suspicion, were it not for the fact that no one was getting to and from the plant in Blanche Point with the winds what they are, and the roads all shut down. You could have easily told me that, except there *had* to be a reason you kept your cards close to your chest. Because revealing that would mean revealing something else."

He couldn't help gloating a bit — he'd even go so far as to say he impressed himself with his cleverness. He reminded himself, however, that the truth was a serious blow to Sherri, who was so fixated on projecting the image of a picture-perfect existence, and so he eased back a little bit.

"I'm sorry, Sher — I do get it. If you'd told me he was home, it would be one thing for him to not get up when a crowd of drunken partiers shows up after midnight, it would be quite another for him not to notice that one came into his room and tore apart the chest of drawers. You would have had to tell me that it's *him* sleeping in the spare bedroom, and I know that was the last thing you wanted to do. You never actually went to the police by the way, did you? That's why you came to me, to try to get this thing settled before you'd have to tell everything to the cops and risk the whole town finding out? You knows how gossipy folks can be."

Sherri's eyes were downcast, but she nodded slowly. "It's bad, Wish. Real bad. We figured we'd give it until the holidays at least, one last go of it, but . . ."

He reached out and took her hand. "Unfortunately, you've got bigger problems here now. So, you went downstairs to let the Mummers in. A crowd come in, and through the jigs and the reels you lost track of who's supposed to be there and who isn't. It isn't your fault — but you did make a mistake when you assumed that the person you saw on the stairs *came in* with that bunch."

Sherri pulled her hands back. "What are you saying? There couldn't have been any one else slip in?"

Wish shook his head. "No, I don't think so. But someone could have come from upstairs to check on all the commotion, and then made a quick retreat when it looked like the coast was clear."

That *definitely* was not what Sherri was expecting. She physically recoiled as though from a blow.

"No. No, no no! Martin and I have our differences and our issues, but he would never be at that. We needs to go talk to the others who was there last night."

Wish smiled a sad smile. "I could be wrong, you're right. But I don't think so. Think about the state of Lisa Tobin's clothes this morning — they've been by the wood stove all morning, and were still damp. You said they made a big mess of water when they came in out of the storm — *in your living room*. Yet somehow the stairs were totally dry?

"Meanwhile, meaning no offence, but it doesn't make a lick of sense for someone to go through your cabinets and take the one thing that looked like it was a piece of junk on string. You never wore the thing or talked about it, and there were plenty of other pieces of jewelry that looked much nicer — and looked more valuable, at that. Whoever went through your things knew what they were looking for, knew what it was, and had enough sense to make it look like a burglary."

"And *why*, pray tell, would Martin want to do something like that?"

"Because he sees the writing on the wall." Wish hesitated for a moment, drew a breath. "Because he sees the divorce coming."

She couldn't help it. Hearing it in plain terms like that

caused Sherri to burst into a sudden crying fit, déjà vu for Wish as he'd stood in Lisa Tobin's kitchen a mere hour earlier. This close to Christmas, he knew this was torture, but knew it would be worse if he didn't finish.

"Lauren Maxwell is a lawyer, so I asked her for a little bit of advice, for a friend-of-a-friend. She allowed that for two old farts, married for a few decades, where one of them looked after the home and reared their daughter while the other one worked rotation work . . . chances are the fella is going to be paying spousal support for the rest of his days. Know what I'm saying? A lot of dollar signs there. Fortunately, his wife has a few nice pieces of jewelry, and surely he's got some sort of claim to half of what she owns, right? Only problem is," and he held up a notepad where he'd quickly scribbled a note, "it's spelled out in the law that 'gifts, inheritances, trusts or settlements received by one spouse during the marriage' don't get divided."

"Meaning what?"

"Meaning when you eventually split up," he said, wishing he had more diplomatic vocabulary in his arsenal, "the law says that you get to keep that brooch all to yourself. That god-awful, ugly, *expensive* brooch. Martin allowed his only hope in being able to retire before he turns 100 was to get his hands on that brooch and sell it, because he was never going to see any piece of it otherwise. When that crowd showed up last night, be musta figured Santa Claus came early, and jumped at the chance to stage a break-in. Until the storm lifts though, I think you'll find your Mother's brooch is still under your roof."

The brooch really was a hideous thing. Sherri LeDrew was making a conscious effort to wear the reclaimed piece around now as much as she could, but Wish couldn't bring himself to say that it was doing her any favours. It especially clashed with her New Year's Eve dress, but she was at least three glasses of wine deep, so that if she'd cared at all when she dressed (which he somewhat doubted) she certainly didn't by that point.

Martin had made his exodus from the house earlier than planned. The turkey was thawed and still had to be cooked, and him coming down with a suitcase while she peeled potatoes over the garbage had to be one of the most uncomfortable moments of their flickering marriage, second only to calling him down just before the Christmas Eve church service to tell him she would keep her mouth closed if she could also keep the house. As she ate her meal in solitude, she couldn't help but wonder how far into the drive Martin would have been when he would have passed the locksmith coming out to re-do the doors (she was more than happy to pay the holiday premium).

It had been a hard year, and an even harder Christmas. New Year's, however, was the time for the possibility of new beginnings, and for moving past those moments in a life that become so stagnant they threaten to suffocate you before you even realize you're having trouble drawing breath. She would realize, sooner rather than later, how lucky she was to have figured out just what sort of a mess she was in before it got to that point. She already realized that she was happier than she'd been in a long time, watching the fireworks on TV in Wish's living room and not caring if she'd still be awake come midnight. At the time of the year when the darkness was the deepest and the coldest, Sherri couldn't help but believe in some warm hope from deep inside of her.

"Thanks again for everything," she said. She turned then from her wine and reached into her oversized purse, drawing up a wrapped parcel.

"Go on girl, you shouldn't have done anything special. I was glad enough to help."

"Be that as it may, I insist," she said, tossing it into the soft recliner where Wish was just starting to nod off to sleep an hour before the community names would scroll across the bottom of the screen.

Wish acquiesced, pulling back the gold foil wrap on a full bottle of dark rum. He was mostly glad it wasn't a companion piece to that brooch.

"Happy New Year," he said, cracking the lid and thinking about what a long day tomorrow might well end up being.

Sharon Hunt

Sharon Hunt was born in St. John's, Newfoundland. Her short stories have appeared in Ellery Queen Mystery Magazine, Alfred Hitchcock Mystery Magazine, Mystery Tribune and Black Cat Weekly, among others. "The Water was Rising", published in Ellery Queen was shortlisted for two international awards, while "The Keeper of All Sins", published in Alfred Hitchcock, was included in *The Best American Mystery Stories, 2019.*

Pineapple Crush and Green Zebras

Betty Patterson was outside early, just past seven, pruning the yellow and white tea rose bushes in her front garden. She and her husband, Gordon, had planted them forty years ago and the blossoms and fragrance never failed to lift her spirits. It was a glorious summer morning: warm but not humid, with a fluttering breeze from nearby Victoria Lake.

She sighed with contentment as she dug in the earth around the bushes.

The maple and silver birch trees on Lakeside Crescent, the small cul-de-sac that she and four other families had called home since their houses were built in the mid-1960s, sparkled in the sun and threw dancing patterns on the asphalt.

The crescent was a picture of peace and contentment.

Most days, that was.

Today though, when she popped her head up over the pickets of her blue fence, she realized something was off; it was the sudden appearance of Nancy Thomson, leaving her yellow brick two-story across the way.

Dressed in pink pedal pusher pants and an oversized white blouse that billowed out behind her, Nancy started jogging across her lawn, towards Betty.

Jogging.

Nancy did not jog.

She wasn't much of a walker either, if truth be told, preferring her beloved Raleigh Sundance bicycle and BMW Mini Cooper, the latter a splurge after retiring two years ago.

"I need wheels under me," she said, in all seriousness, whenever Betty suggested a walk around the lake. "Wheels are more dependable than my aging spindles."

Well, her aging spindles were doing just fine this morning, Betty thought. She, herself, was a runner and impressed by Nancy's smooth and brisk pace.

What didn't impress her was the obvious concern on Nancy's face when she reached Betty.

"Is something wrong?" Betty said, although, obviously, something was because Nancy rarely appeared outside before nine or ten, since she stopped working as an accountant. Now, instead of rushing to spend her days with spreadsheets and calculators, she was usually soaking in the tub at this time of the morning, she once confessed to Betty.

"Followed by a leisurely breakfast and then curling up with the latest murder mystery from my ever growing library."

Betty had laughed as Nancy continued, "I no longer feel the need to be the early bird that catches the worm."

Now, Nancy caught her breath before saying, "I'm

worried about Robert."

"Robert? Oh dear, why?"

As if on cue, they both looked back across the street, at Robert Harris' low-slung, ranch-style house of brown bricks and green trim. Betty considered it the gem of the crescent, the house she and Gordon would have purchased had they moved a bit faster, although she was more than happy with the smaller, tan ranch with blue trim they had settled in.

"Robert is always in his vegetable garden by now. I see him through the bathroom window. You know how devoted he is to those heirloom tomatoes."

"Yes, they are wonderful, especially the Green Zebras. I make his mother's Chow Chow recipe every fall with those tomatoes. It's delicious."

"I do, too. Betty, I haven't seen him in the garden since Saturday. It's now Monday."

"That is strange. Have you called over?"

"Yes, but only this morning. It keeps going to voicemail. On the weekend, I thought well maybe he's just catching up on documentaries. There are some really good ones on PBS now, and I didn't want him to think I was checking up on him."

Betty nodded.

"Last week, he mentioned a new series about Transylvania, focusing on everything but Dracula."

"Yes, I saw the first show last night. It's very good."

"I'm quite worried now that he's fallen or something else has happened."

"Let's go see what's going on."

"Thank you. I was nervous to go by myself," Nancy said.

Robert's front garden was a bit sparce of flowers and shrubs, but that was because his real passion was his vegetables, which took up much of the back garden. In addition to growing award-winning tomatoes, he grew cucumbers, lettuce, and half a dozen other vegetables.

His was the greenest thumb Betty had ever seen, and she considered herself no slouch in that department.

Robert was generous with what he grew too, not only supplying his neighbours with vegetables throughout the summer and fall, but also donating baskets full of them to the local food bank.

After getting no answer at either the front or back door, the women returned to the front.

Robert had given Nancy a key, for insurance purposes, but she had never had to use it until this morning. When she went to unlock the door, she and Betty were both surprised that it hadn't been locked.

"This isn't good. I should have checked on him Saturday," Nancy said, stepping inside.

After calling his name and receiving no answer, they moved through the rooms, all neat, dark and empty. To make matters more concerning, Robert's car was in the garage. He, like Nancy, was not much of a walker, but in his case it was due to arthritis, which had gotten worse over the last few years.

Working in his garden helped keep the stiffness at bay, but any sustained walking made it worse, he told Betty.

"Where could he be?" Nancy said, her eyes welling with tears.

"Let's drive around and see if we can find him. He

might just have gone down by the lake for a change."

"You and I both know Robert doesn't do change. He's a creature of habit."

An hour later, Nancy pulled back into her driveway, having driven around most of Ellisville, which was a small town.

They hadn't seen Robert and were now quite alarmed.

While Nancy went to call the hospital, and then the police, Betty returned to Robert's to look around some more. She felt like they must have missed something the first time through.

Of the five families on Lakeside, Betty, Nancy, and Robert's were the closest. They had more in common than with the others, although the Bergers and Donaldsons were lovely. Betty, Nancy and Robert, though, had lost their spouses within the last three years, and none of those couples had children: by choice for the Thomsons and Harrises, as both husbands had had difficult childhoods and feared turning into a father like their own. The Pattersons had deeply wanted children but couldn't have them and, in the 1960s and 1970s, there were not the medical advances available today. While they had applied to adopt, that hadn't worked out either.

Over the years, the six became good friends, as well as neighbours, going to dinner and the theatre together, playing Cribbage Tuesday evenings and, every few years, vacationing as a group.

Betty stopped in the hall to look at a photograph of Robert and Ruth, their last vacation in Florida, before Ruth was killed in a car accident the next spring. They stood in front of a gleaming white building surrounded by orange and yellow flowers in Key Biscayne. The building housed their condominium which the Thomsons and Pattersons had stayed at often.

Such smiling, contented faces, Betty thought, returning the photograph to the table. Robert had never truly recovered from his wife's death and afterwards spent a lot more time alone.

Nancy and Betty had never truly recovered from their loses, either, although the drawn-out nature of their husbands' illnesses gave them more time to prepare for becoming widows, if you ever really could prepare for that.

Still, the three of them found ways to keep going: Robert with his vegetable garden and the documentaries he loved; Nancy with her mysteries and a new passion for baking; and Betty, with her roses and the custom hats she still occasionally made, after a career making headgear in the costume department of Ellisville's world-famous Shakespearean Festival theatre. The Christmas before she died, Ruth commissioned her to make a Homburg hat for Robert, as he had always loved the curled brim hat that Winston Churchill wore in his famous V for victory photograph.

Now, Betty found it sitting on a shelf in his closet, the left side buckled, as if something had fallen on it. Like her, Robert was fastidious about his belongings. He wouldn't let something remain damaged, if it could be repaired.

She made another surprising discovery in the bathroom: a prescription for him for Exelon, the medication

Gordon had been prescribed five years before he died. It was for mild to moderate dementia symptoms. The bottle was full, although it had been prescribed a week ago.

"Oh, Robert," she said, returning the pills to the medicine cabinet.

In the kitchen, she checked the refrigerator, knowing from experience how important it was for people with dementia to eat properly and healthily. There wasn't much on the shelves besides vegetables: no milk, fish or berries, no whole grain bread. There was, however, a lot of cans of Pineapple Crush, in the cupboard and empty ones in the recycling box. Robert, originally from Newfoundland, loved this soda, an east coast favourite. The high sugar content in sodas, though, could be detrimental and cause greater agitation and rashness; it had with Gordon, until he was weaned off sugar altogether.

How ironic that the two men shared the same diagnosis. When Robert found out about Gordon's dementia, he was one of their most helpful friends, coming often to visit and talk with Gordon, playing cards and helping to keep his mind off of what lay ahead. On bad days, when Gordon left the house and couldn't be found, Robert helped bring him home.

When Betty met Nancy outside, she told her about the prescription and how it seemed that Robert wasn't taking the pills or eating properly.

"Gordon was that way at first."

"Where did he go, when he ran away?"

"To the lake, but it only happened a few times. Then I had extra locks installed high up on the doors, which he couldn't reach and that helped. But then, he would hide in the house, often in closets or downstairs, in the cellar."

"Robert had a new cellar built in the basement last year, because the original one was too small for all the vegetables."

"But we checked the basement earlier."

"We just called out and quickly checked the rooms, but the door to the new cellar is paneled to match the paneling in the room, so it doesn't stick out. Because of the arthritis starting to cripple his fingers, he had the door made so you just push and it opens; there's no doorknob."

They hurried back downstairs but paused before opening the cellar door, agreeing that they mustn't look upset; if he was there, them being upset would just upset him more.

Robert was asleep in a corner of the cellar but woke up when Nancy called to him. He looked around, then at the women, and said, "What am I doing here?"

"You must have been doing something, gotten tired and decided to take a nap," Betty said, remembering what she would tell Gordon, when he would ask the same question.

Never say 'don't you know', or 'don't you remember', the doctor had told Betty. "It will just make Gordon more anxious and upset. Be part of whatever world he is in at the moment."

That advice helped.

When Robert stood up, Betty noticed a half dozen empty Pineapple Crush cans next to him.

"Why don't you get washed up and Nancy and I will

make breakfast for the three of us?"

"That sounds good. I'm really hungry."

While Nancy stayed with Robert, Betty went home and got eggs, whole wheat bread, and a package of salmon steaks she had been planning to cook for dinner.

Nancy met her in the hall. "He brought his prescription bottle, asked if we would mind helping him."

Betty took Nancy's hand. "Of course, we will help him, in every way we can."

Nancy nodded and led the way back to the kitchen.

"I think I will cross the Pineapple Crush off my weekly grocery order," Robert said, before putting a pill into his mouth and taking a drink of water.

"That sounds like a great idea," Betty said.

He looked out the window. "It's a lovely day. After breakfast, I'll get back to my tomatoes. The Green Zebras are almost ready to harvest. My mother used to make lovely Green Tomato Chow Chow. I should give you the recipe."

The women turned back to the counter to wipe their eyes.

Teresita E Dziadura

Teresita E. Dziadura has steadily been making her voice heard in the Newfoundland writing scene more and more over the last two years, making her presence known at NaNoWriMo writing events and seminars as a force to be reckoned with, bringing wit and insight to every conversation she's a part of.

She made her first mark in the world of published fiction with her short story 'Beyond No Man's Land' in *Chillers from the Rock*, a chilling tale that cemented her as one of the fresh new talents in the industry.

Dziadura describes herself as a sci-fi and horror nut, but is also a longtime fan of British comedy. She has studied Marine Biology and has four children with her husband of twenty-five years.

Her first novel, *Corporate Invasion* was released in 2021.

Murder and Mystery-tea

RCMP cruisers filled the parking lot across the street from the Joel Brake Memorial Stadium. A crowd of locals had gathered to watch, piling up on the curb, pressing against the yellow police tape bulging it in while they leaned as far as they dared, craning their necks, in an effort to catch a glimpse of anything. Drawn like flies to carrion by the red and blue lights that reflected off of the windows of nearby businesses.

"What's goin' on here?"

A man with a cigarette hanging from his lips turned to see an older lady leaning far over the tape as she dared lest she tumble over. She was short and slightly plump, with silvering hair pulled into a sloppy bun at the base of her neck and was dressed in a neat floral blouse tucked into dark denim capris over equally bright floral converse. Her clothes were protected by a pale green apron with a steaming teacup on the breast pocket and "Mug Up and Mystery-teas" in a fancy script below it.

"They're sayin' a body was found."

"No." She gasped and grasped at a St. Anthony medal that hung on a chain around her neck. "G'wanwhicha.

They did not. Nothing that interestin' happens here."

"They did. Or so they says. I never saw nuttin' myself."

"That's some shockin'." She turned to the woman who was standing behind her. They could have passed for twins except the other was taller.

"Ger, did you hear that? A murder. Right here in our own backyard." She glanced back at the man. "Figuritively speaking, that is."

"Mary Margaret Parsons." Gertie put her hands on her hips and looked down at her sister. "Can you at least try to have a little respect? Someone is dead."

"Speaking of the dead, can you not sound like Mama?" Mary gave a shudder. "Fine, have it your way. But this will make a great story for the podcast. I can hear it now: 'Mug Up and Mystery-teas brings you, Summer Fest Fatality'; or, maybe The Dance Hall Death?"

The man Mary had been speaking to began to back away from the pair, watching Mary with a wary eye.

"With that reporting you should apply to be a reporter for that rag, the Daily Rail." Gertie rolled her eyes. "We don't know anything yet. Poor soul could have simply had a heart attack."

"Well, I wouldn't do the podcast until we knew." Mary rolled her eyes dramatically, "As the kids say, I'm not a noob."

"Mer, did you ever think that we might have known him or her."

"Of course I did, but if it's a friend, then finding the truth is all that more important. I'll call the station later and talk to Amelia."

"I'm sure she's—"

"Got time to speak with her favourite Auntie? I'm sure she does." Mary turned back to the scene before them. "I'll drop in right after we close up the shop."

"Speaking of the shop, we should open up." Gertie gave her sister's arm a tug.

"Indeed, sister." Mary looked around at the gathering crowd. "We should have a good bit of business today." She turned to follow her sister. "It's been lovely meeting you…"

The smoking man stumbled to a halt, his half-smoked cigarette falling from between his lips. "Umm, it's, ah, Cal."

"Cal, lovely to meet you. You should stop by the shop sometime," She plucked a business card from the front pouch and handed it to him, "Show us that and the first cuppa's on us."

"Umm, thanks. I'll do that." He stepped on the smoldering butt of his cigarette and ground it to a pulp. "The missus—"

The ambient noise from the crowd grew and the trio followed the collective gaze. An RCMP officer and a man both in a too big suit were heading for the crowd. A grin crept across Mary's face. "Oooh, that Melly. You go ahead, sister."

"I'm sure she's got better things to do right now."

"Nonsense. I'm her favorite Auntie." Mary grinned at her sister as she pulled out the small audio recorder she always carried in her apron pocket. "She'll talk to me. She loves me."

Staff Sergeant Williams watched as her officer tucked his notepad back in his breast pocket. The excited hum from the mob reached them, desperate to know what had happened here on this little wooded trail. She looked over his shoulder and peered between a gap in the trees that afforded her a decent view of the hoard.

He followed her gaze. "Quite the crowd, huh."

They looked like meerkats, twisting and standing on their toes to peer over each other's head in the hopes of getting a glimpse of something, anything. Behind them, vehicles had parked bearing the logos from VOCM, CBC, and Saltwire. "The vultures have arrived." She stifled a groan. She let her eyes wander from the vehicles and recognized some of the reporters she'd spoken with in the past. A noise of disgust slipped from her throat. "Have Jake take photos of the crowd."

"In case the killer is there?" He flushed when she gave him a side glare. "Yes. Of course that's why." He added and took out his cell phone and made a call. After he hung up, he looked back at her. "CME is on her way in from town."

"Good, we're gonna need her eyes on this one." Williams' eyes flicked back to him before resuming her watch of the gawkers. She groaned and muttered under her breath. "Three months."

"Ma'am?"

"Nothing."

She walked to the shallow depression where he'd lain. The forensics team were already at work, collecting, gathering like worker ants.

"Town's not gonna be the same without Ray."

"I know. He was a good man. No idea why someone would want him dead. If it was Jack—"

"Speak of the devil." The corporal nodded his head towards the far end of the lane. Williams followed his gaze and her shoulders dropped. "Ugh. How'd he find out so fast?"

A balding man of middle years approached the scene. He reminded Williams of a rhino the way he charged towards them, his oversized grey suit flapping in the breeze.

A crow cawed above them and the corporal looked up. "Spies?"

"Wouldn't surprise me. Politicians do have an almost supernatural ability when it comes to this stuff." She cleared her throat and stood erect. "You really shouldn't be here, Mr. Gooden. This is an active crime scene."

His brown loafers slipped and slid on the slippery gravel, and he had to grab a low branch to stop from landing on his rump. Williams stifled a grin, and the corporal snorted a laugh that he managed to hide behind a cough.

"Really, Captain Williams? When something like this happens in my town, where would you propose the Deputy Mayor be?" He said his title as if it were an honourific as he brushed himself off but only succeeded in smearing turpentine over the front of his jacket.

"Mr. Gooden, it's Staff Sergeant Williams. I'm not a captain."

"Yes, yes." He waved his hand dismissing her. "Now Captain, what in God's name is going on here?" He stomped around the crime scene as he spoke, forcing Williams to grab his arm and pull him towards her.

"Sir, stop. We need to keep the scene from being contaminated."

He looked down at her hand and followed it to her face. "I'll keep in mind just how cooperative you've been when I meet with Patrick next week for golf."

"You golf with Assistant Commissioner Barry?" The corporal blurted. Williams glowered at him and he took out his notebook and began to scribble in it. Williams turned back to the deputy mayor. "Mr. Gooden..."

Gooden glanced at the corporal, then dismissed his existence. "I'm waiting, Captain."

"Staff sergeant," Williams muttered. "Very well, sir, if you insist—"

"And I do."

She bit her tongue to stop what she wanted to say. "A body was found this morning, but—"

"A murder in my town. This is unacceptable! The Summer Fest—!" His voice raised in pitch with each word uttered.

"I never said anything about murder. The CME hasn't made any determination—"

"I overheard you and that fellow there." He waved a well manicured hand towards the corporal.

"That would be Corporal—"

"There goes my "Nicest Town" award."

"Sir, no town isn't immune to the wickedness of humanity, but until the CME report is in, this could be natural." The image of the pristine body, lying just off the path, flitted through her mind, and she knew she didn't sound as certain as she should have.

"Well, what else could it be?" He gave her a withering stare, then walked over to where the forensics team was scouring the ground. "A dead man, in a secluded alley, the night after a popular dance which he attended?"

"Sir, how did you know the deceased was at the dance?" the Corporal and Williams asked in unison.

"It's obvious."

"What's obvious is you continually trying to walk through my fecking crime scene!" That last came out with the snap of command and Gooden froze in place, but she choked on it when she realized what she'd said.

"So, I'm right."

"No. We don't know anything yet."

"Who was it? I've a right to know."

"Mr. Gooden. You can threaten me all you want—"

The voice of Bing Crosby singing, 'It Had to be You' broke their standoff, with the tinny echo of electrionics

"Ray?" Gooden's eyes went wide, and he spun around searching for the source of the music.

The two officers headed towards the alders, dividing to go on either side of the depression.

"It's here." The corporal pulled a neoprene glove from his pocket and used it to reach into the scrub and pulled out the phone. The screen was cracked but it was still working and showed a picture of a woman sitting amongst a flower bed with 'Wifey' below it. The corporal hit the decline button and handed the phone to one of the forensic team who dropped it into a baggie. "Get that looked at, asap."

Gooden looked from the bag to Williams and back

again. "What's Ray's phone doing here?"

"Mr. Gooden, I'm sorry to have to tell you, but our Mayor is the decedent."

He paled and grabbed a nearby tree to steady himself. "Are you certain?"

Williams nodded. "He had his wallet on him."

"Does Cora know?"

"A car is on the way to her now."

"I should go to her." Gooden drew his lips down in what Williams believed Gooden thought to be sorrow. "She shouldn't be alone."

'He looks like an angry mushroom,' Williams thought and had to cough and cover her mouth to hide the grin that itched at the corners. "She won't be alone." Gooden glared at her. "Their son is home. He was with them at the dance last night."

"Nonetheless." Gooden regained some of his composure and brushed his sleeves, flicking at the bits of moss and bark that had clung there. He looked at his hand covered in sticky sap and bark bits. He tried to scrub them off on his trousers, succeeding only in smearing it, creating a matching sticky streak to the one on his jacket.

He swore under his breath. Williams reached into a pocket and pulled out a wet wipe, handing it to Gooden, who grabbed it without so much as a thank you, tore it open and tossed the wrapper on the ground.

"I'll want daily updates. My constituents will want answers." He gave up on cleaning his clothes, settling for getting some of the sap off his hands. He tossed the wet nap onto the ground. The corporal glowered and picked up both the wipe and its wrapper.

Williams sighed. "Yes, sir."

"For now, one of us needs to make a statement. I'd prefer it was me, but I really must get to Cora." He put that simulacrum of sorrow on once again. "Poor, poor woman."

Williams groaned. "I'll talk to them." She gave her kevlar vest a tug pulling it straight, smoothed her hair back, tucking an errant bit behind her ear and set her hat, took a deep breath and her expression slipped to her practiced 'I have to speak to the public' mask.

Williams and Gooden walked down the dirt road towards the parking lot and Wiliams thought, 'Save me from fools and politicians.'

Even from this distance you could feel the energy from the gathered crowd: eager, anticipatory, excited. Her stomach turned. For a moment time shifted and the crowd with cell phones held aloft morphed to medieval peasants holding torches and surrounding the gallows. Their mutters of curiosity echoed through time to cries for blood, foaming at the mouth for a death, any death, as if death was a spectacle and her mask slipped for a second revealing the disgust she felt before she regained control. She shook her head, and the twenty-first century returned.

"Captain?" Gooden added.

"I'm fine. Just getting a headache."

The older man nodded. "I suspect it's not the last one you'll have."

"Nor do I."

As they drew closer, she let her eyes flick over the crowd. Looking for anyone that might seem out of place, too calm, or too nervous, or too invested. Her eyes fell on the smiling visage of her Aunt Mary and she missed a step. Her mask of neutrality slipped again and she groaned.

"Captain? Do I need to call in someone to replace you?" Gooden said.

She glowered and nodded her head towards Mary. He followed her gaze to the frantically waving Mary who was yelling their names loud enough to be heard over the din. "Oh God." Gooden's groan echoed Williams'. "Of course she's here."

"Yeah." Williams let out a string of oaths under her breath. The deputy mayor added a few of his own.

Williams took a deep breath, held it, and let it out slowly. "I should have expected her." She spotted the grim face of Gertie behind the eager Mary. "Them." She gave her vest another tug. She looked at the crowd and thought, 'Fecking disrespectful killer. Thousands of kilometers of woods and coastline in Newfoundland, but they had to dump the body less than forty meters from the Parson sister's shop.'

"Yes, well then, I'll leave you here, Captain." Gooden looked at his watch. "I left my car at the Town Hall." He dropped his voice so only Williams could hear him and with a final glance towards Mary who was frantically waving at them. "Good luck." Then trundled off towards the waiting reporters. His expression was one of business-like sorry as he spoke to them, "Thank you all for your patience. Captain Williams here will bring you up to date." He looked back, gave her a thumbs up, ducked under the police tape, and headed towards the nearby Town Hall.

"Still a Staff Sergeant," she growled under her breath before turning to address the waiting crowd who met her with questions that tumbled one over the other in quick succession.

"Was there a body?"

"Where is it?"

"Whodff was it?"

"How'd they die?"

"Please, everyone, this is just going to be a very brief update and I won't be taking any questions at this time." She raised her hand, quieting the cacophony to murmurs and whispers. "Right now, all I can say is that the body of an, as of yet, unidentified male was found behind the area after last night's dance. No cause of death has yet been determined and there will be no other information until the family is notified. If anyone has any information, please reach out to the RCMP or Crime Stoppers."

More questions followed but one voice rose above the rest, "Staff Sergeant? Staff Sergeant? Miss Williams? Amelia? It's me, Mary, your Auntie Mary. Could I ask you a few questions?" The short woman waved her little recorder above her head. She bullied ahead through the throng, pushing her way to the front like a rhino on a mission. No one stood a chance. They parted like the Red Sea, letting her pass lest they get a jab of her bony fingers or elbow in their ribs. "Amelia, it's for the podcast."

"Mary," William's voice was terse. "I've nothing else to say. You will be given the exact same information at the same time as the actual press."

The press turned to watch the exchange, interested in the woman who'd so drawn the Staff Sergeants attention or ire.

Mary recoiled and looked hurt. "But…"

"No buts, Miss Parsons. I suggest you attend to your shop." She pointed down the street. "It seems you have customers waiting. For a change."

Mary turned and saw Gertie opening the door and letting the patrons in. "Oh dear." She scurried back through the crowd undeterred by Williams' visible annoyance. "I'll call you later, Amelia." She gave Williams a wave, brushing off the slight.

'Of course you will,' she thought. She turned back to the media and realized they'd caught the entire exchange. Williams stifled another groan and suspected she'd be doing a lot more of that before this whole mess was done. She addressed the media: "A press release will be sent out when we have anything else. Everyone else, go home. This isn't a spectator sport." Only some heeded her orders and she turned away in disgust.

She headed back to the scene, keeping her back straight and her head high, but when she was out of sight of the crowd, she let her shoulder droop. "Well, that's gonna be on the five o'clock news."

"What is?" The corporal rejoined her.

"Did you see that disaster?"

He shook his head.

"Mary and her infernal, ridiculous podcast. The headlines are gonna read, "RCMP Detachment Commander bullies little old lady." She pinched the bridge of her nose again. "Ugh."

"Were you really that hard on her?" They stepped between the trees and the cool shadows swallowed them. "Everyone knows how, well, intrusive, those two are."

"Yeah, maybe but she's my mom's best friend. I've

known her since I was born."

"Oof."

"Yeah. Oof. She was alright until she discovered podcasts." She could almost hear her mother's disappointed tone when she would receive the inevitable call later. This time Williams didn't bother to stifle her groan. "I'll call and apologize later. Right now, we've a job to do."

Morning arrived and Mary sipped her tea and watched her sister over the rim of her cup. Gertie was drinking her morning coffee and toast while reading the news on her tablet.

"Anything interesting?"

Gertie raised her brow. "Well, they're tracking a hurricane down by Hati. There's a new play at the LSPU hall in town. Another stabbing on George Street. Oh, and the city has moved the homeless camp, again."

"The news is always so depressing." She took a too-casual sip of her tea. "Anything more local?"

"Mer, you have a tablet of your own."

"It's dead."

"Mmhmm." She scanned down the news website then froze, her mouth drawing tight. "Summer Fest is pushing ahead in the wake of tragic news. Mayor Ray…" Gertie's voice was tight when she spoke. "It was Ray."

"Ray?"

Gertie nodded.

"Did they say how?"

Gertie read further. "Under investigation. I'll call Murray's Funeral Home later and get the time of the wake and funeral. We will be attending." Mary shrugged. "And I'll order flowers later and have them sent to Cora." She made a low gasp. "Oh Cora, the poor thing. She must be inconsolable." Gertie laid her tablet down. "They have that big fiftieth coming up next month. Cora was in the shop just the other day. She was so excited, telling me all about the cruise Ray'd surprised her with. St. Martin, Puerto Rico, Antigua…"

"Hmm, I wonder if she'll go alone?"

"Mary!"

"What? I was just thinking' she might sell the tickets cheap…"

"You're incorrigible."

"I'm practical." She drank the last of her tea. "Speaking of practical. I'm going to head to the RCMP detachment after breakfast."

"We've got the shop to run…"

"It's a Monday. Should only be the usual crowd and I won't be long."

"Mer—"

Mary stood and put her mug in the dishwasher, grabbed her keys. "It's for the podcast."

Williams held the preliminary report from the Chief Medical Examiner.

"Pending the tox screen, a fecking heart attack." She slapped the paper down.

"Atrial fibrillation, to be exact." She glared at the corporal and he shrugged. "I read it."

"Ray was a health-conscious man with no pre-existing

heart problems. CME is suspicious, so when she called me to say she'd sent the prelim over, she told me she's gonna screen for everything."

"Everything?"

"Yep. No way was this natural. Heart attack victims do not fold their hands across their chest and cover their own faces with a hanky."

"That would be pretty unusual."

"Any word from trace on the hanky?" She tossed a photo of the handkerchief onto the desk before the corporal.

"Not yet, ma'am. I'll check back with them later today. DNA will take a bit, but if there's anything else—"

A loud knock came on the door, and it opened. "Good morning, Melly!" A colourful sprite appeared in the doorway carrying a tray of teas.

The corporal looked at Williams with a smile twitching at the corners of his lips and mouthed, 'Melly?'

Williams replied, "Do not speak of this." And made a finger gun and shot her officer. His grin broke free and spread across his face.

"I left a tray at the front desk with a bag of cream and sugar." Mary addressed this to the corporal.

"Thanks Mis P." He slipped from the room and a last look in saw Williams glowering at him. His phone chirped and when he looked there was a text with, I'll remember this.

Williams turned her attention to her sudden visitor. Mary laid a cup on the desk before Williams. "Your favourite."

The comforting smell of a London Fog reached Williams, soothing her frayed nerves. "Thanks, Auntie Mer."

"I saw the news…"

"I figured that's why you were here." Williams looked at the woman who sat before her. The quirky, odd, eccentric little woman whom she'd known her whole life. "I'm sorry about yesterday."

"Pish posh. You were working and I was, well, foolish."

Williams grinned. "You can be taught."

"How the worm has turned. There was a time when I taught you but that's been, as the kids say, a hot minute."

Williams laughed. It felt good and pulled some of the tension from her shoulders. "Anyway, I'm sorry. I know how much Mug Ups and Mystery-teas means to you." She took a drink of the tea. It was good. Mary did have a way with tea. "Mmmm, this is good."

"Thanks. It's my own blend."

"You're getting good." She put the cup down, "Now, what can I do for you, Auntie Mer?"

"Well, I was rather hoping we could talk about Ray…"

"Auntie Mer, you know I can't."

"Just a hint?" She pulled out her little pocket recorder and pressed the red record button.

"Fine. But off the record and you can't publish the podcast until after I make my official statement. You can have it ready to go and hit post the second I finish, but not before. Deal?"

Mary nodded vigorously. "Have you determined the cause of death?"

"Not yet."

"Any suspects?"

"Everyone."

Mary made a face. "Any incriminating evidence?"

"We're waiting on forensics to do their thing. Until then…" Williams shrugged.

"I guess it's too early?"

"Yup. Frustrating, isn't it?"

"Quite." Mary stood and put the recorder away. "Sorry to have bothered you, Melly." She glanced down and saw the crime scene photos. She turned one towards her. He was still wearing the clothes he'd had on at the dance, navy blue trousers with a white button up shirt, sleeves rolled up to his elbows. A blue and white napkin or handkerchief covered his face. "Oh Ray. Who did this to you?"

"That's what we're gonna find out, Auntie Mer."

Gertie led the way into the city hall office with a large box of pastries in her hands, Mary following with several carafe of tea and accouterments. "It's the right thing to do." Gertie had said while she flipped the open sign to closed. "They are our customers, our friends. We'll drop in on the Town Hall first, since they're around the corner, then Cora. Kindness never goes astray." Gertie could be overly kind, in Mary's point of view, but she tagged along. This was where Ray worked and lived.

The receptionist welcomed them in and sent the pair upstairs with their offerings. They got off the elevator. 'This place is an homage to seventies architecture,' Mary thought as they made their way down the white hallway over grey industrial carpet. 'All the personality of a box.' It always left her longing for her cute little Victorian cottage with its English garden. They stopped before a set of plain wooden doors. A painted plaque with Mayor on it was its only adornment.

Gertie shifted the balance of the boxes and lifted her hand to knock, but Mary brushed past and pushed it open. "Afternoon, Gloria."

The middle-aged woman looked up. Her eyes were red and puffy, but she managed a weak smile. Gertie put a full box of pastries on the desk while Mary handed Gloria a cup of her favourite tea, a simple chai latte.

"Oh, gods that's good." She reached in and took out a danish.

"You should be home."

"I'd love to, but Jack called me in."

"What?" the sisters said in unison.

"Yeah. Told me there was no time to rest. That, and I quote, "We're public servants, Gloria. Our constituents need us. Ray would want this.""

"Wait, he used Ray?"

"Yeah—"

The door opened and Jack stepped inside. "Oh good, you made it in."

"This poor woman should be at home—" Gertie started in her best principal voice.

"Nonsense, Gert. We are here to serve."

"Labour law mandates—"

Jack held up his hand. "Please, do not lecture me on labour law. I am a lawyer after all."

"Mary, it's okay." Gloria turned her gaze to Jack. "What, Jack?"

"I'm going to need you to reschedule that zoning vote."

"Again? You dragged us all—"

"It would be disrespectful to hold a vote today."

"There shouldn't be a council meeting at all." Mary glowered. "You've become hard, Jonathan Gooden."

"It's a hard world, Miss Parsons."

"And people like you make it harder." Mary looked at her sister with pride. Gertie wasn't one to speak out.

"Gloria, send out the email please." He grabbed a butter tart from the box, took a cup of tea from Mary, and gave them a polite nod. "Ladies." The door shut with a snick.

"He's such a pompous ahhh—"

"Mer…" Gertie warned, nodding her head towards the exhausted admin. "Go home, Gloria," she told the other woman.

"I will. As soon as I send this email." Gloria clicked away at the keys of her laptop. "Done." She looked up at Mary. "This whole rezone has been a thorn in my side for weeks. Such a stupid thing for friends to fight over. Some stupid rezone for Waverly Development. Jack wanted it, Ray not so much."

"Jack must be…"

Gloria's smile was sad. "Yes. I'm sure he is."

Gertie drove while Mary mulled. "Sister, I can't help but think this land thing may have something to do with Ray's death."

Gertie was quiet before responding. "Cliche but not

improbable."

"I'm glad you think so. Any chance you could distract Cora?"

"You don't suspect Cora?"

"Like Melly said, I suspect everyone. But no, not really. I just want a minute or two in Ray's office. There might be something…"

"Fine. But be quick." Gertie pulled up in front of the beautiful historical home where the couple lived. A small dog ran from the front porch up to the gate, yapping at the pair as they headed towards the home, treats in hand.

"Bela, it's nice to see you too." Mary patted the terrier and pushed the gate open, blocking his escape with her leg. Bela escorted them through the garden that wrapped all the way around the house. Ray and Cora would hold an annual tea party here every Canada Day. The last one had been catered by Mug Ups and Mystery-Teas. It was always perfect, but today Mary saw a patch of disturbed earth along the front porch: plants in bedding pots and tools were dropped haphazardly around, as if the gardener had been snatched mid-work. 'Must have been where she was when the RCMP officer came to get her.'

Gertie lifted her hand to knock. This time the door opened of its own volition instead of Mary plowing ahead.

"Gertie? Mary? What are you doing here?" Cora flicked her hand and Bela ran to sit by her feet, his little tail wagging enthusiastically and a happy doggy grin on his face.

"We're here to pay our respects."

"Oh, thank you. Come in."

The three set up in the sunroom, with a fresh breeze blowing in off of the river that ran behind the house. The conversation was pleasant, generic, talking of anything other than Ray.

Mary kicked Gertie under the table. "Here, Cora, let me help you clean up."

"Thank you. I'd appreciate that."

Mary thought Cora looked exhausted. "Might I use your restroom?"

"Certainly, you remember where it is?"

Mary gave a nod and headed into the main house, through the dining room and down the short hall where the guest bedroom, bathroom, and Ray's home office were. Mary pulled the bathroom door shut and slipped into Ray's open office. His laptop was on the desk along with a brown manilla envelope. She flicked the folder open with the back of her nail. Ray's will. A quick look through showed that Cora was the primary beneficiary, including all of Ray's assets and his share of a holding company, along with their son who was gifted a cottage, Ray's classic cars and so on.

"Interesting…" She took out her cell phone and snapped a few pictures of the will before turning her attention to his laptop. She didn't have gloves on her so she used a kleenex from Ray's box to cover her finger. "No password? Ray, you were too trusting." She clicked on a file, and it opened. "Well, lookie at this." She used her phone to take more photos then slipped from the room. She opened the bathroom door, flushed the toilet, rinsed her hands and rejoined the others. They'd made their way to the foyer.

"Thank you for coming." Cora gave each woman a polite hug before opening the door. "It means a lot."

"Of course," Gertie responded. "If you need anything…"

"I appreciate that." She took out a handkerchief from her pocket and dabbed at the corners of her eyes.

Mary glanced from Cora to the handkerchief to the flowerbed. Cora saw her staring and stuffed her hanky into her pocket.

"I'll have to do something about that before the… The…" Cora swallowed hard.

"If you'd like, I can pop over and finish that for you?"

"I can't ask that of you."

"It's no problem. You know I love to garden."

"It really isn't necessary."

"I insist." Mary stepped back up one step.

"Oh well, I guess then. Umm, sure. I have to go out today. Funeral home. Tomorrow would be better."

"Tomorrow it is."

She waved them off, Bela running back and forth between her legs.

"We're gonna have to keep an eye on her."

"Cora? Seriously?"

"Yes, Cora. But first?" She held up her phone. "This."

Cora's errands were brief, the dog groomers where she dropped off Bela, then the funeral home, the grocery store, back to get Bela, and then home. They parked down the street and waited.

"While we wait, let's look at these." Mary plugged

her phone into her laptop and brought up the photos that she'd taken. "Look at this, Ger." Mary pointed to the will.

"Yeah, I'd expect to see Cora as beneficiary."

"Not that." She pointed to a section of the will. "This. CarGood Holdings. Ever hear of it?"

Gertie shook her head.

"Well, this might help." She scrolled on to the pictures.

"Well dang. Et tu, Brute?"

"And now we wait."

Night folded in around them. One by one the lights in the homes flicked off.

"This is ridiculous. I'm starving and have to pee. Ray and Cora were the perfect couple."

"Outward perfection often hides a rotten core."

"Ugh. I hate when you get all philos—"

"Look!" Mary slapped her sister's arm and pointed. Cora's BMW was backing out of the driveway. "Now where would she be going at this hour?"

"A drive? Normal people will do things like that when stressed."

"Just follow her."

Gertie rolled her eyes but pulled out and followed as Cora took the on ramp and headed down the Trans Canada Highway. They passed town after town and Cora drove on. "Are we gonna drive all the way to St. John's?" As Mary spoke Cora's left indicator began to flash. "Go past then turn and come back."

Gertie muttered about stupidity and fools errands, but complied.

"It's the road to the old Brassville dump."

"Why on earth would Cora come here?"

"I can think of a few reasons." Mary patted Gertie's arm. "Pull in there. We can walk the rest of the way."

They ducked into the bushes when they heard the crunch of tires on gravel. As the car passed, they could see Cora's face. She was grinning.

"What's she got to be so happy about?" Mary glanced back at Gertie.

"You know, Mer, I think we should check out that dump."

Williams paced in her office. The CME had said she'd call before the end of the day, and it was getting late. The phone rang and she dove for it and hit the speaker phone so she could continue to pace. "Staff Sergeant Williams."

"Good evening, Staff Sergeant. It's Bev."

"Thanks for getting back to me so fast."

"No problem. This is turning out to be interesting."

"How so?"

"Well, I got the tox report back."

"That was fast."

"A friend owed me."

"What did you find?"

"Ray was well soused. Blood alcohol of point one-one."

"Guess he enjoyed the dance, but that wouldn't kill him."

"Nope. The rest is clear except for one thing."

There was silence as Willliams waited for Bev to continue.

"Digoxin."

"Digoxin?"

"Yep. Ray was poisoned."

Williams flopped down into her chair. "Poisoned? Are you sure?"

"I am."

"How?"

"It was in his blood and stomach. So, he ingested it. Along with wine, hor d'oeuvre from the dance, and tea."

"Bev? How would you get a lethal dose of digoxin into a person while in a public space?"

There was a pause while Bev thought. "Me? I'd spike his drink. Need something pungent to offset the taste, so a mixed drink or a strong tea or flavoured coffee would do it."

Images of Mary grinding herbs, flowers and tea leaves, filled Williams' head. Of her aunt filling small pouches with the fragrant mixes while recording episodes for her precious podcast.

Williams looked at the paper cup with its steaming teapot logo that was on her desk. "Oh, Auntie Mer, what did you do?"

"We should call Melly." Gertie insisted for the hundredth time. The white kitchen garbage bag sat in the middle of the table.

"We can take a peek." Mary pulled on a pair of gloves they used in their shop and pulled back a piece of the bag.

"We shouldn't." She leaned in next to Mary, trying to get a look. "What's in it?"

"That clinking noise is a brown bottle, a paper cup with the Summer Fest logo, there's a receipt from Fannies

Flowers, can't quite make out what's on it—" Mary shook the bag and gasped. "Ger, there's a hanky in there."

"So?"

"Same hanky I saw on Ray's face at the police station and the same on that Cora used to dry her crocodile tears."

"We've got to get this to Melly."

A knock came on the door and the two jumped. Gertie answered and found Williams at the door. "Oh, Melly. We were just talking about you."

"You were?"

"Come in, please. You want some tea or coffee?"

Williams shook her head. "Mornin' ladies. I was surprised to find the shop closed."

"We were going to the wake."

"I don't think that would be good, right now."

"Why?" Gertie asked.

"Well, I need to ask you both some questions."

"About what, sweetie?"

"Ray's murder."

"Oh?"

"Yeah. You were at the dance, right?"

"We were." Both sisters nodded. "Did you bring any of your teas with you?"

"No. Why would we? Everyone had pre-bought drink cards. Tea, coffee, and food was free."

"Hmmm."

"Melly, what are you getting at?" Another knock on the door made everyone look. This time, Williams answered and the corporal was standing there.

"No foxglove ma'am."

"Any other nightshade?"

"No. Mostly herbs and a few edible flowers and vegetables."

Williams sighed with relief.

"What are you getting at, Melly?" Gertie was getting angry and it showed.

"I'm sorry, but we got some information, and I thought maybe that Auntie Mer…"

Mary laughed. "You thought I was the killer?"

"Why would Mer kill Ray?"

Williams looked sheepish. "Podcast fodder?"

Mary fair roared with laughter while Gertie looked indignant. Mary stood and walked over to Williams. "Sweetie, if I killed someone, you'd never know it."

"With all the true crime you listen to I wouldn't be surprised."

"Since you're here, we have something to show you."

"What?"

Mary lifted the garbage bag. "This."

It ended with a body. It always did. This one was still living, unlike Ray.

Mary and Gertie drove up the road from their house.

"We should call Melly and tell her everything." Gertie pulled her phone from her pocket.

"She's gone after Cora; we're going to follow the final piece of the puzzle. Once we confirm it, we'll call her"

Mary pulled up into one of the parking spaces before the brick building. "He'll likely be in his office."

The receptionist waved to them as they walked past

him to the elevators. The elevator doors opened with a bing and the ugly industrial carpet muffled their footsteps. They were passing the mayor's office. The outer doors were open, but the office was closed and muffled voices came from inside.

"A man and a woman?" Mary sounded excited. "I wonder who it could be." Without a moment's hesitation Mary pushed the door open.

The room was moderately sized with a sofa, chairs and a large wooden desk that looked like it had just stepped out from a 1980's magazine. Behind it sat Jack Gooden while Cora faced him, blocking the sisters from view.

Mary clicked record.

"Jack, I'm telling you, they know."

"How the heck would they figure it out? They're just two old biddies who think they're Sherlock, but in reality are a pair of Lestrades."

"You know that Lestrade always made the arrest for Sherlock, right?"

"Not without Holme—"

The door burst open, Mary and Gertie stood there, arms crossed. "Lestrade? Really, Jack? At worst we're Doctor Watson." She stepped over the threshold. "I'm very disappointed in you both."

A selection of emotions flicked over his face, before he settled on shocked indignation. "My dear ladies, I think you misheard." He stepped from behind the desk and walked towards them. Gertie took a step back, but Mary held her ground.

Cora gripped her skirt in both hands. "It's not what you think."

"Really?" Gertie asked. "Then what is it?"

"Jonathan William Gooden." Mary's voice snapped like a whip and he hesitated. "The little boy I taught in kindergarten would never have done this."

"That little boy is long gone."

"Apparently." Gertie sounded like the disappointed Nan. "Greed."

They all looked at Mary. "You heard me. Greed. The lust for money and power."

"And how did you come to that conclusion there, Sherlock?" That last was said with a sneer.

"Neither of you are as smart as you think." Gertie glowered.

"The murder weapon is on its way to the RCMP lab."

Cora stepped forward. "That's not possible."

Mary chuckled. "Oh but it is. We followed you. Once you dumped the bag, we could take it."

"No." Cora leaned against the desk for support.

"That means nothing. I'll say you were with me the whole time."

"Please, do." Mary rounded on Jack. "I mean it's not like you're the other fifty percent shareholder in it? Nope, not you. That would mean you and Cora now own it."

"Bul—"

"Just don't, we saw the minutes from the council meeting. We've got proof that you wanted to sell that prime bit of land by the river, but a condition of the sale was that it needed to be rezoned." Mary grinned; Gertie sounded like she was enjoying herself.

"That proves nothing!" Cora snapped.

"Doesn't it?" Mary asked.

"It proves motive." Gertie added, "Ray was blocking it."

"He was having it designated a wildlife refuge. If he had, no sale."

"No money."

"All circumstantial."

"Is it?"

"You really think I'd kill my husband for money?"

Mary laughed. "If you'd listened to my podcast, then you'd know people have killed for less."

"And you both had two point five million reasons."

"He was robbing me and our son of our futures!" Cora snapped.

"There was other land."

"Nothing like that."

"But he'd be alive." Gertie was appalled.

"Enough." Jack waved a dismissive hand. "If you had any solid pro—"

"Then we'd call the cops?"

"Yeah."

"Done." Mary was cackling with glee and even Gertie was grinning.

"What?"

"They're on their way upstairs. We were just sealing the deal." Mary pulled out her recorder.

"You—" Jack's face was blood red. He reached into his pocket and pulled out a revolver.

Cora and Gertie gasped while Mary's face grew dark. "You think that will make things better?"

"It'll make me feel better."

"So one life sentence isn't going to be enough for you?"

There was a commotion in the hall and Williams appeared. "Got your text." Her eyes flicked to Cora, then to Jack and the gun.

"Don't," she ordered.

Jack looked around. All his bluster was gone. Fear and resignation filled his eyes.

"It's over, Jack." Cora put her hand on his arm and lowered the gun.

Williams and her team took the gun and placed it in an evidence bag, put the pair into cuffs and escorted them past the sisters. "You're under arrest for the murder of Ray Collins."

Mary handed Williams her recorder. "Don't forget my exclusive for the podcast."

Cora was fighting back tears, "What happened Jack? It was a good plan."

"It was." Jack pulled away in a final act of impotent defiance: "And we'd have gotten away with it if it hadn't been for those crones."

Williams rolled her eyes. "We'd have gotten you without them. Eventually." Turning to her officers she ordered, "Take them away." She watched as the other officers took Cora and Jack away and breathed a little easier.

She looked back at the sisters. "What am I going to do with the two of you?"

"Take your two favourite crones to lunch?" Mary linked her arm into Melly's and Gertie took the other side.

Melissa Bishop

Born and raised in the Mount Pearl area, Bishop is a newcomer to the genre fiction scene in Atlantic Canada whose fantastic prose has taken the provinces community by storm. Her work won three Kit Sora awards: July 2019 'Cycles,' September 2019 'Huntress of the Woods,' and May 2020 'Brightest and Best.' In addition she has placed numerous other times.

Writing about her story 'The Photograph' in *Pulp Science-Fiction from the Rock*, R. Graeme Cameron of Amazing Stories wrote: "This is a classic SF tale... Possibly a reminder that things aren't always what they seem."

Bishop describes herself as a loyal Tolkien fan who enjoyed reading about different mythologies as a child. She currently works as a high school teacher, teaching at the same high school she attended in her youth. She started writing when she was very young and honed her skills in high school, when she started a pen pal friendship that has lasted for over 17 years, writing stories back and forth to each other.

In May 2023 she released her first novel, *The Fairies of Foggy Island*.

Book Club

Fog swallowed the town. It crept across the coastline around noon, trailing long, wispy fingers across the ragged shore of the community nestled within its sheltered bay. By evening, the clouds had woven their way down every crevice so that anything more than three feet in front of you was a wall of white mist. Any traveller unaccustomed to the place would have long retired to one of the two bed and breakfast spots. Agnes, however, had lived in the town for seventy-two years and toddled through the vapoured laneways like she owned them.

She hadn't far to travel. Up the bend, round the corner and there it was: the amber glow of a singular shop at war with the grey weather. The store's steps were few, but Agnes took her time on them, wondering if each creak came from the well-worn wood or the groaning objection of her own bones. Catching her breath on the landing, she rested her hand on the doorknob. Turning it, she was enveloped in warmth and bombarded with a symphony of scents: cinnamon, nutmeg, and bread baking in the oven. A brass bell above the entrance jingled, announcing the final customer for the evening.

"Lock the door, Agnes," a grainy voice replied behind the small counter and display case. There stood a woman with her back to the door, attention fixed on the glass pane of a large stove. Her ashy grey hair was pulled back into a tight bun. Her thin fingers twisted the dial of a timer clasped between her hands.

"You still have customers, Ester." Agnes' eyes shifted to the two men sat at a corner table littered with papers. Their florescent jackets, folded over a free chair, were a foreign sight for the small town.

"Ah, it's alright, Agnes. I told the constables they could finish their work here. You know Amelia's Inn got no common room and we're here for a few hours yet."

Agnes' wrinkled cheeks turned up a warm smile at the gentlemen. One looked fresh to the force, brown hair and barely in his twenties. His uniform was without a single wrinkle. The other was older, with an authoritative air the young one had not yet learned. They nodded to Agnes before she turned to the only other occupied table, one across from the officers, where an animated chatter was emanating.

"Took yer time, Agnes!" a woman with tight grey curls and green eyes chided. "You get lost in the fog or what?"

"I told ya' both there'd be weather, didn't I?" smiled another. Her light brown hair held wisps of white, giving the semblance of butterscotch ice cream. "My knees were *aching* the past few days and my knees are never wrong!"

"Wallace was late for supper," Agnes explained, pulling back one of the empty chairs and easing herself into the seat. Her frame filled up the space, and another groan — perhaps her back, perhaps the chair's — followed her excuse. "He was helping poor Edgar at the funeral parlour. Edgar's son threw his back out this week of all weeks."

A pall passed over the group's mirth.

"Oh, bless Wallace's heart," the butterscotch-haired woman replied, bringing a withered hand to her chest. "And such sad news about Arthur."

A resounding hum of agreement circled them before settling back into an awkward silence. Ester, finally satisfied with the bread baking in the oven, moved to take up the final seat.

"Sad news to be sure," she agreed, lowering her voice and nodding in the direction of the officers. "That's why those two are here. Filling out reports."

"Why?" The butterscotch woman's eyes went wide.

"They do that whenever someone dies suddenly at home, Doris. Just to make sure there's nothing suspicious," Ester explained, rubbing her right wrist and rotating it.

"Oh, well that's good. Though a lot of work for the poor lads to come out here in all this fog. I mean in our little town? Poor things." There was a small hesitation before Doris asked, "How did Arthur die?"

"You're a terrible gossip, Doris!" Mildred, the green-eyed granny growled, staring down Doris before shifting her sights to Agnes. "Well out with it, Agnes. What was Edgar saying about it?"

"Said Arthur fell down the stairs," Agnes replied, accustomed to Mildred's surly attitude.

"What a sin." Doris shook her head. "An absolute shame."

"It is." Ester strummed her fingers on the table. "In

more ways than one."

"What do you mean by that?"

"Well," Ester leaned in, trying to be quiet but failing in a shop so small in size. "You remember the garden party back in August? Well, Marvin Wilkins was having a grand ol' chat with Arthur — laughing and all excited. Something about Arthur leaving a portion of his estate to the town. Wanted to get Marvin's opinion on the idea, since he's the mayor and all. You know how the council has been trying to make some changes, with all the tourists wanting to stay here and sightsee nowadays."

"A portion of Arthur's estate!" Doris exclaimed, eyes bright. "Why, he's worth millions! That'd set the town up for ages!"

"I wonder if Arthur went through with it?"

"That's the thing, Agnes," Ester explained. "Marvin was here today for tea and a biscuit. Apparently, he was meeting Arthur here on official town business. A pile of papers with him. Waited for ages, but Arthur never showed. Finally, Marvin left."

"From what I hear, Marvin was the one who found him," Agnes added.

A low whistle echoed through the almost empty coffee shop.

"That'll be the kettle." Ester rose with some effort, stretching her back as she stood to her full height. "Would you like a cup, lads?" she called to the officers as she moved. Their eyes were already fixed on the women. The younger man smiled and shook his head, the older seemed keener on Ester's conversation. "Alright then, just for us. I'll be right back, girls."

The conversation continued as the baker busied herself behind the counter.

"What a way to go," Mildred muttered, clicking her knitting needles together as she worked on her newest project.

"And so unlike Arthur too," Doris noted. "You remember when we all took samba classes at the community centre? When Ellen's girl was home for a stint? Arthur never missed an evening!" She chuckled, moving her arms from side to side as if to mimic the dance. "He could samba up a storm!"

"He was pretty nimble for an old fella." Mildred's knitting needles clicked away. "Strange for him to lose his footing on the stairs. Suppose he slowed down since then."

"But he walked all the time." Agnes scrunched her nose. "The whole town knew that. He was constantly out and about. He'd always stop for a chat." A pause. "And now that I think of it, last time I was at Dr. Martin's office about my hip, I saw her chatting it up with Arthur. He'd just finished his appointment and I remember the doctor saying he was 'fit as a fiddle' for his age!"

Murmurs of agreement resounded round the group. The two officers eyed one another. The younger slowly produced a notepad from his belt and flicked to a blank page. Retrieving a pen, he began scribbling some notes. The chatter continued at the other table.

"It's such a shame for Arthur to go like that. All alone." Ester returned, setting a cookie tray and teapot down for her friends. "With him being such a part of our community and all."

"Well, if I were Arthur, I'd rather die alone than have that son of his around." Mildred pearled another piece of yarn, glowering. "Charlie Prachitt is one sly creature. If ever there was a father and son like chalk and cheese, it was Arthur and Charlie."

"You would think the boy'd be grateful. Arthur handed over the business when he retired. Millions that company makes. But does Charlie thank his father? No. Does he visit? Hardly at all! And the city only forty minutes away!"

"Twenty with the way Charlie drives!" Mildred grumbled. "I've watched him zip along my street with that fancy car of his in the past. Don't slow down for nothing."

"Oh, that seems the way everyone drives nowadays — always in a hurry," Doris nodded. "Sure take last night! Margaret's boy, Tommy, almost got ran over walking home from the O'Driscoll's. A car came speeding through the pitch black! Didn't even see him!"

"You don't say? Is he alright?"

"A bit shaken but otherwise fine. Could have landed in a ditch and not a soul would have known until morning!"

"Did he see the car? Get the license?"

"Wasn't able to. Just screeched up behind him and was round the corner before he knew it. Such a strange thing."

"Shockin'."

"Well, I'm glad Tommy is okay." Agnes poured herself a cup of tea, the steam curling upwards from the heavy ceramic cup. She did the same for them all. "He's a nice boy, unlike that Charlie Prachitt." Her eyes moved from one old friend to the next. "According to Edgar, Charlie isn't going to be here for his father's funeral. When Edgar called him with the sad news, it was like Charlie wasn't even listening. At first, Edgar thought he might be in shock, but Charlie was just plain cold. Claimed he was busy. Taking some business trip out of country tomorrow morning."

An exclamation rose from all round.

"Of all the...ungrateful..." Mildred stammered, her face crimson. "What a way to react to your own father's death!"

"Can you imagine?" Doris was dismayed. "I mean, to miss your own father's funeral? After everything Arthur did for him?"

"It ain't right," Mildred growled. "A son like that should be locked up with the key thrown away!"

"Well, no matter what his son is like, Arthur was an amazing man," Agnes offered, toasting her tea in the air. "Kind and generous. Would have done a world a good here if only he had lived a little longer."

"Yes," Ester sighed. "I certainly can't imagine Charlie honouring his father's wishes and helping out the town."

"Perhaps Marvin can speak with him. Tell Charlie what Arthur had planned to do for this place. It's where Arthur was born and raised, after all."

"Oh Dorothy, that's giving Charlie too much credit." Mildred scowled at her knitting, fingers furiously moving. "You heard how he acted when he found out Arthur was dead. And if Charlie had known anything about Arthur meeting Marvin here today? Trying to leave money to the town? He'd have put a stop to it. He'd have driven right down here to tell his father off. It's the way he's always been when money's involved. Remember how Charlie acted when his father donated five thousand to the school? Charlie nearly flipped his lid!"

"Yes, he was livid," Agnes agreed. "I sincerely doubt Charlie would part with any money, no matter how much or what his father's wishes were."

Ester exhaled, stirring a tarnished spoon about her tea-cup. It clinked along the edge as the tea and milk swirled. "Perhaps it's for the best the town don't see the money. All those tourists might be trouble after all. Though my little shop could use a few more patrons."

"I suppose you're right, Ester." Doris lifted a lemon square between her fingers and took a bite before continu-ing, "I mean, tourists can be trouble too. Always taking those selfies. Sometimes in the most random places and times. And, you know, some of them don't respect prop-erty at all. Sure, I woke up this morning to find my bego-nia's beaten down! Looks like someone trampled them. Mud all over the white fence Frank just painted, like they were trying to climb it."

"Did it…look like they were going into Arthur's yard?" Ester inquired.

"Well, now that I think of it — yes. And Frank did no-ticed damage done around Arthur's property. Some of the lattice was broken up along the side of Arthur's house — close to the second story window. He was going to talk to Arthur today and see if he needed a hand repairing it. We figured a cat had tried to climb up it."

"Doris…that would have to be a fair size cat to be breaking parts of the lattice like that."

"I s'pose you're right, Agnes. But what else could it be? Vandals?"

The chatter died away once more. The only sounds that remained were the clinking of spoons against ceramic cups and the speedy scribbling from the officer across the room.

"Alright, alright, enough gossip." Mildred broke the quiet with her curtness. "Let's get to this month's book." She turned, finally setting aside her knitting needles and fishing something from the fabric bag that hung on the back of her seat.

"Oh, give me a moment, Mildred," Ester said rising. The older officer was motioning her over. "I think the constables want something. And the breads got two minutes left. I'll be right back."

Chairs scraped along the floor as each searched their purses for something. Agnes retrieved hers first — a well-worn paperback with a dark blue cover. Police tape trailed across the front. She crinkled her nose. Her grey eyes scanned the depicted crime scene on the cover.

"Wasn't a fan of this read," she flatly stated.

"Well, I certainly wasn't reading another one of your romances!" Mildred spat, slamming down her copy sternly.

"You can say all you want about my romances, Mildred, but these murder mysteries? With all these elaborate plans?" Agnes huffed her disapproval. "Nonsense! And the detectives? So unrealistic. You wouldn't solve a murder like that! Putting all those tiny pieces together."

"As if you'd know," Mildred retorted, picking up her knitting needles once more.

Ali House

Ali House is an award-winning, bestselling author, originally from Newfoundland. She is a graduate of the Fine Arts program at Sir Wilfred Grenfell College (MUN), and currently resides in Halifax where she works in arts administration and spends more time than a person should in and around theaters. She is a master storyteller whose work has helped define the landscapes of science-fiction, fantasy, and horror writing in Atlantic Canada.

House's short fiction has appeared in the *From the Rock* anthology series, *Bluenose Paradox, Kit Sora Artobiography,* and *Terror Nova.* Her short fiction was collected in 2020 in *The Lightbulb Forest.*

Previous novels include *The Six Elemental* and *The Fifth Queen,* both a part of her creator-owned *Segment Delta Archives* series. Other works include the fantasy series *Choose Your Own Adventurer,* the *Santa Claus Protection Program,* and *The Island Adventure* as a part of the Slipstreamers series of novellas, and *Variety Show.*

In April 2024 she released her eigth novel, *The Hunters and the Hunted.*

Exit Pursued By Murderer

- Scene 1 -

Outside, the snow was coming down fast and furious.

"I knew we shouldn't have bothered coming in," Star said, flipping her long, bottle-blond hair back with one hand.

"Wasn't exactly our choice," Carrie muttered as she stared out the window. In the darkness, every streetlight showed a thick cascade of flakes. Snow covered everything, hiding trees and cars under a blanket of white.

"At least we're safe inside and still have power," Ryan added cheerfully, smiling at the other two.

Star and Carrie both turned to her, giving her matching unimpressed looks. They'd both rather be at home, happily heeding the weather forecaster's blizzard warning, but their director, Wilson, had called the warnings an overreaction and refused to cancel today's rehearsal. Anyone who refused to show up would instantly be fired and replaced — and everyone who knew Wilson knew that her threat wasn't a bluff.

The weather had been deceptively calm as everyone

made their way to the theatre that morning, and they'd wondered if maybe the forecast had been a bit too harsh, but while they'd rehearsed, the snow and wind came in with a vengeance. By the time someone looked out a window and realized how bad it had gotten, it was too late. They were stuck here.

"CAN WE GET BACK TO SCENE TEN?"

Wilson's voice bellowed throughout the auditorium, causing the three actors to jump and quickly turn away from the window. The director was standing in Row E of the orchestra, her hands on her hips, glaring at them as if they'd missed multiple warnings that the break had ended (they hadn't).

Daria, the stage manager, was looking at Wilson with her mouth half-open, but then she closed it without saying anything, slightly shaking her head. She'd worked with Wilson before and knew that it'd be best to not rock the boat now and simply apologize to everyone later.

Looking around, she noticed that Hannah, the playwright, had shrunk in her seat in Row G, sitting so low that it looked like she was trying to disappear. Their lighting, sound and set designer, Jo, was further back in Row P, but Daria could see the frown on her face. Then Jo shook her head and went back to her notes. She'd also worked with Wilson before.

"We've all seen snow," Wilson continued bitterly, jabbing her finger angrily in the direction of the stage. "Scene. Ten."

The three actors turned away from the window and obediently made their way down the aisle and onto the stage. Sure, this was only a profit-share show, but none of them wanted to give up the opportunity to be on stage and perform in front of tons of people. Maybe one day Wilson would get repercussions for her terrible behaviour, but today she was still in charge.

Star and Ryan took their places — centre stage and upstage left, respectively — while Carrie disappeared into the stage left wing.

"LIGHTS UP," Wilson bellowed.

Although the lighting on stage didn't change, the actors promptly started the scene. Star launched into her monologue, gesticulating with her hands as words poured from her, a pleading look on her face. Ryan said nothing but watched intently, her eyes focused on the lead actress.

Barely two minutes had passed before Wilson was on her feet again. "STOP! Stop everything!"

By the time Star stopped speaking, Wilson was already halfway to the stage. Star sighed loudly and crossed her arms. Carrie peeked in from offstage.

"I've told you a hundred times," Wilson bemoaned. "You've got to be *sadder* at this point. This is your terrible backstory you're revealing, not a take-out menu." She motioned for Star to move aside, which Star did (after rolling her eyes), moving as far upstage right as she could get. Carrie disappeared into the wings again while Ryan got back into character.

"I want a spotlight here," Wilson demanded, staring at Jo as she pointed up at the grid above her, where the lights were hung. Jo nodded and made a note, adding the spotlight to her current lighting design. Daria also made a note in her script about the newly added spotlight, hoping that one day Wilson would learn how to *ask* for something instead of demanding it.

Taking Star's place centre stage, Wilson put a tormented look on her face and launched into a melancholic (and worse) version of the monologue. Daria noticed that Wilson was drifting from the centre stage mark, where she'd instructed Star to remain for the whole monologue, but made no comment on it. Wilson did whatever Wilson wanted.

She was seven lines in when a creak was heard above the stage. A few eyes glanced up to the grid, wondering if maybe the storm was causing the old theatre to settle incorrectly, but Wilson refused to be distracted from her acting and continued the speech.

In fact, the only thing that could stop Wilson was the large Fresnel light plummeting from the grid.

- Scene 2 -

Daria stared at the stage, her brain refusing to comprehend what she'd just seen. The streak of black falling from above; Wilson dropping to the floor; the crunch and crash as the light smashed into the stage; Wilson's body lying prone.

Time seemed to stop as everyone stared at the scene. The theatre was so silent that the only noise was the howling wind outside.

Daria's brain suddenly clicked on. and she propelled herself from her seat, rushing toward the stage. The lack of blood seemed to be a good sign, and when Daria found a strong pulse on Wilson's neck, relief flooded her body.

One second later, Wilson's eyes flew open. "What the hell?" she asked before wincing in pain and raising a hand to her head. Her right arm bumped the shattered remains of the light and she tried to turn, but a wave of dizziness hit her and she had to stop and close her eyes.

"A light fell," Daria replied in a calm voice. "How are you?"

"How should I know?" Wilson snapped at her.

Daria assumed this meant that Wilson would be fine, but she didn't want to risk it. Unfortunately, they'd never get to a hospital with all this snow, nor would an ambulance be able to get here.

"Van!" Daria called out. The stagehand appeared from the stage right wing, her eyes wide with shock. "Help me get Wilson to the dressing room."

The rest of the theatre was silent as Van came over and helped Daria lift Wilson from the floor. Wilson complained the entire time they carried her to the room, but Daria expected nothing less. She knew that she'd also have to deal with Star's complaints about them putting Wilson in her dressing room, but it was close and right behind the stage, unlike the other dressing rooms which were downstairs. Besides, Star's dressing room had a chaise-lounge, and Wilson needed to lie down.

"You feeling okay?" Daria asked once Wilson was lying on the chaise.

"As good as I can after a damn light fell on my head," she muttered. "I'm going to kill Jo."

"Jo didn't drop the light on you," Daria said.

"Jo's in charge of lighting, so it's her fault."

"Yeah, but she was only in the grid once, earlier today, to make sure the layout she was given was correct."

"Well, she should have spotted that one of the lights

was ready to tip."

Daria decided to stop arguing. "I need to get back. Van, can you stay and watch her?"

Van's eyes widened in fear.

"Ugh," Wilson groaned, putting a hand to her head dramatically. "I don't need to be watched like a baby. I'd rather everyone get out and let me have some peace and quiet."

They didn't have to be asked twice. Daria and Van quickly exited the room, although Daria knew she'd check in throughout the night.

"Thanks for helping," Daria said, and Van nodded.

As Daria made her way back to the stage, she heard Star's voice.

"I mean, that totally could have killed me! If Wilson hadn't stepped in, I'd be dead right now, because I was standing right under that light."

"It was an accident," Jo said, exasperated. "Something must have snapped or broken."

Star huffed. "I wouldn't put it past one of you to cause an 'accident'. I know what you say about me behind my back."

Daria quickly stepped onto the stage, putting out her hands to stop anyone from saying anything that might cause the situation to get worse. "Star, now's not the time. It was an accident, that's all. It's going to be a long enough night without infighting."

Star huffed and tossed her hair over her shoulder, but she didn't say anything else.

"Wilson seems to be okay," Daria said, filling every-one in on the director's health. "We need to keep an eye on her, just in case, but I don't think it's drastic. Still, when the weather clears, we should get her to a doctor."

Everyone nodded.

"So, I guess rehearsal is officially over, but we're stuck here until morning." She looked around and shrugged. "Try not to break anything or blow any fuses, okay?"

The others dispersed, searching for places to charge their phones or avoid other people, leaving Daria alone in the auditorium. Letting out a sigh, Daria looked down at the destroyed light lying in pieces on the stage. She knew that it was an accident — just a terrible, unfortunate accident — but Wilson or Star could have been badly hurt. The only thing that stopped this from being worse was the fact that Wilson had been off-centre.

Suddenly her eye caught on something. Kneeling down, she took a closer look at the wreckage. Lying on the ground was the safety wire that should have stopped the light from falling if the C-clamp loosened its grip on the pipe. Obviously, the wire hadn't done that, but Daria could see no reason why not. The wire was perfectly fine, with no breaks in it. Even the carabiner was undamaged.

Was it possible that the safety wire hadn't been attached? It would be extremely irresponsible of the theatre to not follow proper safety protocols, especially before renting the space. She should get Jo to take a look at all the other lights in the grid, just in case any more were damaged.

Her eyes moved to the C-clamp and she paused. There was something about it that seemed wrong. She looked harder before suddenly putting her finger on it. There was no screw. It was unlikely, but not impossible for the screw that went through the top of the clamp and affixed it to the pipe to loosen over time. If it hadn't been moved or checked in a long time, it might slowly start to twist, until it lost hold on the pipe. That's why all lights had safety wires.

However, if the screw had loosened normally then it would still be in the C-clamp. The metal was thick enough that it'd be sticking out but still on the threads. But there was no screw. Had it gotten knocked out when it hit the stage? Daria looked around, but there was no screw to be seen.

An uneasy feeling settled in her stomach.

After a quick glance to make sure she was alone, she walked into the stage right wing and toward the small, spiral staircase in the back corner. As she climbed, she told herself that she was being ridiculous — that she was overreacting. But then suddenly she was standing in front of the spot where the light had been, looking at a long, solitary screw lying in the metal walkway.

The realization sent a shiver down her spine. It wasn't an accident. Someone had deliberately removed the screw from the clamp and unhooked the safety wire. Someone had tampered with the light so that it would crash on the stage, right on the spot that Star had been standing.

Someone had tried to kill Star and had nearly killed Wilson instead.

Someone in this theatre.

Someone she was stuck with until the storm passed.

- Scene 3 -

After coming down from the grid, Daria decided to

find a quiet place where she could do some thinking. The auditorium was still empty, but there were too many entrance points, and she didn't want to risk having someone sneak up on her.

Grabbing her script and backpack, Daria headed up to the booth. It was a small room with large windows facing the stage, two chairs, and a long table with a lighting board, a sound board, and plenty of room for scripts and coffee cups. Sitting at the table, she took out her laptop, opened a new word document, and began typing.

FACTS:

• Someone deliberately removed the screw from a light and likely unhooked the safety line, ensuring that the light would fall from the grid.

• The light was positioned right where Star would be standing, and if Wilson hadn't interrupted, Star would have been directly hit by the light.

• It would be too risky to do this in advance, as the light could fall at any time, so the person who did this must have done it today — ergo they're a part of the show and are still in the theatre.

• The person who did this might try to hurt Star again.

• If the person does try to hurt Star again, it would mean that they don't care about hurting anyone else, which means we're all in danger.

• Nobody else seems to suspect that this was intentional (except for Star, but that's mostly for attention).

• If I want to figure out who did this, I can't trust anyone.

• I'm going to need to solve this mystery before Star or anyone else gets hurt.

Frowning, Daria stared at the last two lines. Maybe she was overthinking all of this. Maybe it was a weird, unexplainable accident. Surely nobody in this play would try to harm another person.

Except...

Except that Star wasn't exactly the nicest person, and she tended to frustrate people, but she kept getting hired in shows because she performed well and got good reviews.

Maybe someone was tired of working with her. Maybe someone hated working with her so much that they'd rather put her in the hospital.

Daria sighed wearily. She should do something. She *had* to do something. It was her job as the stage manager to make sure that the show went on, and apparently this now meant trying to stop someone from attempting murder.

She should be able to trust Star, but the thought of telling her about all of this and having to deal with her during a serious investigation made her frown even harder. Yeah, it was pretty easy to imagine someone wanting to drop a light on Star, even if the idea of actually going through with it was much harder to picture.

Saving the document as 'Thoughts', she opened a new spreadsheet and created columns titled 'Name', 'Motive', and 'Capability'. It was as good a place to start as any.

Name	Motive	Capability
Star	None (intended victim).	N/A
Wilson	Doesn't think Star is 'acting correctly' and sometimes laments that Star will ruin this show, and possibly her directing career.	Seems cutthroat, but doubtful she'd do something like this. Also, doubtful she'd get onstage knowing that a light could come crashing down at any time.
Carrie	Might get the lead roll if Star was incapacitated.	Don't think she's actually capable of doing this. Was with Star and Ryan during the break, so when would she have 'fixed' the light?
Ryan	Might get a better role if Star was incapacitated.	She's too nice to do something like this. The niceness could be an act, but if so, it's a really convincing one.
Jo	Star has been very opinionated about the set design (along with everything else), which annoys Jo.	Had plenty of opportunity to muck about in the grid, but Jo has dealt with much worse actors.

Name	Motive	Capability
Emily	Star has been very opinionated about the costume designs for her character.	Emily has also dealt with worst actors, and if someone really annoys her, she usually just sticks them with pins 'accidentally'.
Hannah	Star has complained about the script not being good many times, while Hannah's in earshot.	Seems too timid to actually murder a person.
Van	Star has been rude and dismissive toward her.	Seems nice enough and a hard enough worker. Doesn't seem like she's capable of murder.
Me	None. I've definitely dealt with worse actors, and Star isn't my biggest problem on this show.	I know I didn't do it, nor would I risk going to prison for something so stupid.

When she was finished, she read through everything. These motives were all high school stuff; there was nothing here that would get someone mad enough to drop a light on a person and potentially kill them.

Did someone have a deeper secret — something they were hiding and stewing over, building resentment about? How was she supposed to uncover something like that? She wasn't a real detective with time to snoop around everyone's personal lives. Besides, most of them had worked on enough shows together that they all knew everyone's dirty laundry — like who dated whom; who hooked up with whom; etc.

Maybe she should consider who had the opportunity. The light was most likely tampered with during the break. Everyone knew which scene they'd be starting with, and that it was the scene where Star stands centre stage for ten minutes.

Daria tried to remember where everyone was during the break, but it had been twenty minutes, and everyone had a habit of wandering around. Also, even though it was a break, Daria had been busy making notes and prepping for the next scene. She knew Wilson had been next to her the whole time, and that the actors usually stuck together, but other than that, she wasn't sure where anyone else had been.

Sighing, she wondered what to do next.

What did detectives do? They gathered evidence and then started interrogating suspects. She doubted that she'd find any more evidence, so maybe it was time to start talking. If she was careful about what she said and didn't voice her concerns, maybe the perpetrator would let something slip.

- Scene 4 -

When Daria came down from the booth, Jo was at the back of the auditorium, pacing intently. Daria wondered what she was doing, since she'd seemed fine earlier. Was it possible she was beating herself up because the light she'd rigged had fallen on the wrong person!?

Daria frowned at the thought. She didn't like how suspicious she'd suddenly become of everyone. Unfortunately, until she figured out who sabotaged the light, she'd have to stay suspicious.

"How's it going?" she asked Jo as she approached.

Jo looked up at her, worry etched into her face. "Wilson can't fire me because of this, right? I only went in the grid once this morning, and I didn't touch anything, I swear." She put her head in her hands. "I should have checked the clamps and lines while I was up there. What was I thinking? What if it had fallen on Star? What if Wilson had been injured worse?"

"It was an accident," Daria replied compassionately. If Jo was pretending to be concerned, she was doing an admirable job. "Don't beat yourself up. If anything, it was the theatre's fault for not making sure things were properly secured before letting us in, right?"

Jo frowned. "I should go up and make sure the other lights are secured properly, right?"

Daria wondered if this was an opportunity for Jo to get rid of any evidence. She resisted the urge to put her hand in her pocket, where she'd stashed the incriminating screw that she'd taken from the grid. Then again, if Jo had wanted to get rid of the evidence, she could have gone up to the grid while the auditorium was clear. She wouldn't have needed to waste time pacing or beating herself up.

Jo paused. "Wait, what if I say everything's okay and nobody believes me? What if none of them trust me?"

"If we can't trust you, then we can't trust anyone," Daria said. She watched Jo's face for any sign of irony or wickedness, but there was only concern. She smiled. "Personally, I know I'd feel much better if you checked on the remaining lights."

Smiling, Jo thanked her before taking out her wrench and heading backstage.

Her wrench. Daria paused for thought. In order to loosen the screw, someone would need a wrench, and wrenches weren't just lying around the theatre. There was a toolkit in the booth, and both she and Jo had personal wrenches they used, but nowhere else carried a wrench. She'd notice if someone had been messing about in the booth, and she really didn't think it was Jo. Maybe this was premeditated and the perpetrator brought one from home. Had anyone been carrying a wrench today that didn't normally have one? She couldn't think of anyone.

Another piece of the puzzle. She just wished that she had any idea where it went in the big picture.

There was nobody else in the auditorium, so she headed to the lobby. Peeking through the doors, she was surprised to find Hannah sitting in one of the lobby chairs, looking out at the snowstorm. As Daria approached, Hannah turned to her, surprise crossing her face at Daria's appearance. Then her face went back to neutral and she turned back to the window.

"How're you doing?" Daria asked as she took a seat near Hannah.

Hannah frowned and sighed. "This show is going to suck, isn't it?"

Daria paused, surprised by the topic of conversation. "I... Um, I think art is subjective and each person has their own reaction to..."

Hannah's frown deepened.

Daria switched gears. "Jo's done a great job with the set and lights, and Emily's costumes are always amazing, and—"

"The sets and costumes and lights can only do so much. If the audience can't connect to the characters, then it might as well be a recitation of the phone book." Hannah put her head in her hands. "Why did I agree to this?"

"Because your script is good. And Wilson saw that, and she can afford to fund it."

Hannah stared out the window. "I guess."

Daria fought the urge to shake her head. What was it with certain artists and their constant need for validation? "Look, even if things aren't perfect, most people who see the show will recognize that the script is good, and that other people made choices about what to do with it. Audiences are smarter than you think."

"I guess."

The frown remained on Hannah's face, but Daria didn't have time to play therapist — she had a murderer to catch.

"At least nobody was seriously hurt in the accident. That could have caused a real problem for the show."

"Yeah..." Hannah said, her voice trailing off. "I guess it could have."

"We're really lucky Star wasn't in her usual spot. She's got great instincts as an actor. I know everything seems tenuous now, but if you wait until opening night, you'll see her 'forget' most of Wilson's directions. She'll make sure that the show's great and that people connect to her character. You just gotta have faith and be patient."

Daria was laying it on pretty thick — although what

she said about Star 'forgetting' directions she didn't like was true. She watched Hannah, to see if any guilt or surprise made an appearance (that she might have tried to kill the person who could make her show better), but there was nothing.

"I guess," Hannah replied.

It was obvious that she wasn't going to get any more out of Hannah, so Daria decided it was time to call it. "Jo's going to double-check all the lights," she said with a reassuring smile on her face. "So no more accidents."

Hannah turned to her and finally managed a small smile. "That's good to hear."

Daria stood up and headed back into the auditorium. Two suspects down — four to go.

- Scene 5 -

Daria found Carrie, Star, and Ryan in one of the downstairs dressing rooms. Star was sitting on the counter, going on and on about how that light could have killed her, and Carrie and Ryan were patiently listening. Well, Ryan was patiently listening, while Carrie sat in a chair and scrolled on her phone, but neither were stopping Star's tirade.

Neither seemed to be disappointed that Star was still alive either.

"We're acting in a deathtrap! This whole place could fall apart around us."

"Hiya," Daria stepped into the dressing room, waving hello. "I just wanted to let you all know that Jo's up in the grid, making sure the rest of the lights are secure and safe. And, honestly, I'll probably be up there once she's done to do a double-check."

"Thanks," Ryan started, before Star interrupted her.

"Good," Star said bitterly. "I'm glad someone's doing something about this. I swear, if one more thing happens, I'll burn this place to the ground."

"Bit of an overreaction..." Daria muttered.

"Thanks for telling us," Ryan said to Daria, finishing off her thought. "It's hard enough rehearsing without worrying about things falling from the grid."

"Although," Carrie smirked, "I know all of Star's lines, if something does happen and you need to me step in as Vivian."

Star glared at her. "How dare you."

Carrie burst out laughing. "Oh please. Wilson would never let me be lead. She'd hire someone off the street before giving me that part."

"Don't say that," Ryan said.

"We all know it's true."

"But you still don't have to admit it. I'm sure you'd do great as Vivian." Ryan quickly paused. "I mean, not as good as Star, of course, but still great."

Star rolled her eyes, but she seemed happier.

"But Margo does have the funnier lines, and you're so great at delivering them," Ryan continued.

Carrie smiled. "Thank you for the ego boost."

The tension had dissipated, and Daria figured that she'd gotten all she was going to get — at least, while the three of them were in one room. She gave them one last warning to stay off the stage until everything had been declared safe, and left.

She hadn't gotten much from that interaction, but

maybe it was enough for her to rule out Carrie and Ryan. Carrie's comment about Wilson hiring someone off the street before giving her a better role was right. Wilson was particular about actors and wouldn't give someone a better role if she thought they weren't 'right' for it. And while Star had more lines and drama, Carrie's character was more fun to play.

And Ryan. Dangit, Ryan just seemed too nice. Daria couldn't believe that someone like Ryan would be so concerned about Star's feelings after trying to smack her with a light.

It was annoying that Daria wasn't finding the culprit, but at least she was crossing people off her list.

The next logical place to go was wardrobe, to speak to Emily. She had no idea where Van was, so she looked into the other dressing room on her way, but nobody was in there. It was her first time working with Van, so she knew her the least and wasn't sure where she'd find her. This was a problem, since Van was slowly rising to the top of the suspect list.

When she peeked in at wardrobe, Emily was busy stitching buttons onto a shirt.

"How's it going?" Daria asked.

Emily didn't bother looking up. "Good. Heard some rumblings about someone trying to kill Star — and, honestly, get in line — but other than that..."

"Yeah, you kinda missed all the excitement."

"Well, Star's been going on long enough that I think I can piece together what happened." She finally looked up. "How's Jo? I know she'll be blaming herself, even thought I'm sure it wasn't her fault."

Daria noted that the concern in Emily's voice sounded sincere. "She's up there now, checking the rest of the lights. And Wilson's resting in Star's dressing room, but I'll keep an eye on her."

Emily nodded. "Thanks for keeping an eye on everything. Don't worry, I'll give Devin a piece of my mind the next time we're speaking. Can't believe the lights weren't checked before he rented the place. I've half a mind to tell everyone I know in the business. Can't have lights falling on anyone because someone's too lazy to do proper security checks."

Her impassioned speech surprised Daria, but considering how many times Emily had worked in this theatre, she wasn't wrong. Mistakes like that were dangerous and people should know. Unfortunately, it wasn't Devin's fault.

"Maybe hold off on that for a minute," Daria said. "It might have been an honest mistake."

Emily frowned at her. "Why would you..." She trailed off and then a look of understanding crossed her face. "Oh. Nevermind, I get it." She smiled and turned back to her buttons. "Just know, it's not Jo. I've worked with her enough. This show isn't anything special."

Daria froze for a second. Crap. Emily had figured it out.

"I'm not sure what you're thinking," Daria began, but Emily cut her off.

"Don't worry, I'll stay out of your way. I've still got twenty buttons to sew on." She gave Daria a smile. "Good luck."

Daria tried her best to smile back and left the wardrobe room. She had a feeling that she could trust Emily, but it didn't make her feel good that someone had realized what she was up to. What if another person overheard that? What if the person responsible overheard and realized that she was on to them?

Glancing around the hallway, she didn't see anyone. Emily hadn't spoken very loudly. In fact, the only person she could hear was Star, who was now discussing local actors (not in this show) who would have loved to drop a light on her head.

There were only three other rooms in the basement — a washroom, the props room, and the cleaning closet. Daria assumed that Van wouldn't want to sit in a closet with the brooms and mops, so she headed to the props room. Sure enough, Van was in there, sitting at the table in the centre of the room, her head in her hands.

"How's it going?" Daria asked. Even though she kept her voice gentle, Van nearly jumped out of her skin.

"What? Huh?" Van looked at her with panic in her eyes.

Daria put her hands up, as if calming a spooked animal. "Sorry, I didn't mean to startle you. I'm checking up on everyone. That light falling was pretty scary."

"Yeah." Van seemed to settle down a little, but her face still registered shock. "I mean, I didn't see it, because I was at the prop table in the back corner, so I wasn't facing the stage, but hearing it was bad enough. And seeing the mess..."

Daria nodded. "We were really, really lucky that nobody got hurt."

"Yeah..."

"Anyway, I wanted to let you know that Jo is checking the rest of the lights, but you should stay off the stage until she's confirmed it's safe."

Van nodded, but it seemed to be more to herself.

Daria started to turn, but then stopped. "Hey, Van. Is everything okay?"

"Huh?"

"You seem a little... off."

Her eyes widened. "No. I. Um... I have to take a call." She jumped off her chair and hurried out of the room, leaving Daria with a confused look on her face.

Daria wondered if she should go after Van. Her actions were suspicious, which put her right at the top of the suspects list. Her comment about being in the back corner during the time of the accident was a little too detailed. It also put her next to the stairs, and with that corner being so dark, she could have easily sneaked up there during the break. Also, as a stagehand, it wouldn't be suspicious for her to have a wrench. Yeah, she was definitely top of the list.

But why would Van want to hurt Star? As far as Daria knew, this was the first time the two had met. Sure, Star could rub people the wrong way, but Van wasn't going to get far in life if she tried to kill everyone who was mean to her.

Daria looked back into the room and her gaze fell upon the table in the middle. There was something on it. Stepping into the room, she realized that she was looking at a copy of the script for the show they were working on. Except... something was different. Where it said 'Version VI' was crossed out and 'Version VII' was written above it.

Carefully, Daria started to turn the pages. On almost every page notes had been added to the script. There were tons of additional stage directions and character notes.

At first she was confused, but then she realized what she was looking at.

"Oh no..."

She stopped turning pages and picked up the script. She knew exactly what had happened.

- Scene 6 -

After making a quick call, it took Daria about twenty minutes to gather everyone in the auditorium. She had to run around most of the theatre, but luckily almost everyone was where she'd first seen them, and Van was found with Hannah in the lobby.

They all seemed confused — probably because she'd just finished checking on everyone — but Daria explained that she had something important to say and that she only wanted to say it once. She may have used a bit of her 'stage manager authority' to get everyone to agree to congregate, but she didn't want anyone sitting out. She'd even gotten Wilson out from the dressing room.

Once everyone was in the auditorium, Daria stood in front of them. She took a deep breath.

"So, I know you're all wondering why I've gathered you together, but it's for a good reason." She paused. "See, I know that the light falling wasn't an accident."

A few people exchanged looks.

"I knew it!" Star exclaimed.

"The safety wire wasn't connected, and the screw had been removed from the C-clamp. This means that someone tampered with the light, intending for it to fall on someone."

A few people started to talk, so Daria raised a hand to silence them all.

"I had a good long think about it, trust me. Why would someone loosen a light right where Star was supposed to be standing? Why would someone want to drop a light on Star?" Daria paused again. "Except that was the wrong question."

"Excuse me?" Star said, looking offended.

"It took me some time to figure it out, but it wasn't Star that they wanted to drop the light on." Daria held back the smile that she wanted to give. "The person wanted to drop the light on Wilson."

There was an audible gasp from the audience. Daria was pleased, although a bit annoyed because the loudest gasp was from Star, and it was mainly because she was annoyed at not being the main character anymore.

"They knew that Wilson would likely interrupt Star and show her how she wanted the scene performed. They were counting on it. And they were counting on us to be too distracted to notice someone creeping up into the grid to loosen the screw and send the light falling down."

Daria looked at the others. Emily looked intrigued, while Jo, Carrie, Ryan, Wilson, and Hannah were confused. Star looked offended — but that wasn't a surprise. Van, however, had guilt all over her face.

"And the person who plotted it all..." Daria paused dramatically. "Was Hannah."

Everyone turned to the playwright, who's expression turned to shock.

"What?" Hannah turned to everyone, her eyes wide and wild. "What do you mean? It wasn't me!"

"Well, you didn't drop the light," Daria said. "But you planned for Van to do it. Pretty terrible thing to do to someone, make them an accomplice to attempted murder."

Van looked even guiltier and sunk in her seat.

"No," Hannah insisted. "I had nothing to do with this. You can't prove that I did."

"Except," Daria reached into her bag and took out the script she'd found in the prop room, "I have a motive." She held up the script for all to see. "I found this in the props room when I went to speak to Van. It's our script, but a newer version. One with a lot of notes written in your handwriting." She stared at Hannah. "A lot of notes that go against Wilson's directions."

Hannah glared at her before turning to Van and giving her the look of death.

"You knew that Wilson wasn't directing your play the way you wanted and it made you angry. Unfortunately, Wilson's loaded and she's the only one who can afford to produce this. But a production wasn't good enough for you. You wanted perfection. And the only way to do that was to get rid of Wilson and take over directing yourself."

"Shut up!" Hannah yelled. "I didn't do it! I'm innocent!"

Daria looked at Van, who tried to sink lower.

"Yeah," Daria said, "you're totally not innocent. But luckily, the police — who have ski-doos — will be here any minute, and they can decide what to do with you."

Hannah stood up and looked around frantically, as if trying to decide where to run to. But then she noticed that all eyes were on her and she seemed to deflate.

"I just..." she muttered. "I just wanted this show to be good..."

A silence fell over the room as everyone stared at Hannah in disbelief. In the distance, Daria could hear sirens.

Daria shook her head. "Hannah, this show could have been good. But I guess now you'll have to settle for it being notorious."

Cozy Mysteries

FROM THE ROCK

EDITED BY ELLEN CURTIS AND ERIN VANCE

Newfoundland is a place steeped in intrigue, where even the smallest of towns harbour big secrets. What is hidden in quaint libraries, what rumours are spilled over a cup of tea, and what sordid scandals result in mayhem are all revealed by nine sleuthing authors.

From the editors of the From the Rock anthologies comes a new selection of stories, carefully curated from some of Newfoundland and Labrador's favourite authors. Curl up, get cozy, and be sucked into the mysteries that emerge from a rich backdrop of Newfoundland settings, from the furthest flung outports to jellybean row.

Including the work of Ali House (*The Hunters and the Hunted*), Nicole Little (*Roxy Buckles and the Flight of the Sparrow*), Melissa Bishop (*The Fairies of Foggy Island*) and more!